"Open the door, Nance!" Fletcher shouted.

"I don't want to talk to you," she said firmly.

"If you don't open this door by a count of five, I'm going to start singing 'Roll Me Over in the Clover' at the top of my lungs!"

"You wouldn't dare."

"One . . . two . . . I would definitely dare . . . three . . . four . . ."

She flung the door open, and he pulled her to him and lifted her off her feet, carrying her into the house and kicking the door shut behind him.

"What do you want, Fletcher?"

"You're beautiful in the moonlight, Nance. It's pouring over you like a silver waterfall."

"Fletcher, I don't want you anymore. It's too late," she said, but her voice was trembling.

"That won't work, you know," he said, pulling her closer to him. "Love doesn't go away if you ignore it, deny it. It's there in your heart, in your soul. It's a burning need inside you, a need to be one with that person. Are you burning, Nance?"

"Stop it, Fletcher," she murmured, struggling to escape his grasp. But it was too late.

He kissed her. . . .

WHAT ARE *LOVESWEPT* ROMANCES?

They are stories of true romance and touching emotion. We believe those two very important ingredients are constants in our highly sensual and very believable stories in the *LOVESWEPT* line. Our goal is to give you, the reader, stories of consistently high quality that may sometimes make you laugh, sometimes make you cry, but are always fresh and creative and contain many delightful surprises within their pages.

Most romance fans read an enormous number of books. Those they truly love, they keep. Others may be traded with friends and soon forgotten. We hope that each *LOVESWEPT* romance will be a treasure—a "keeper." We will always try to publish

LOVE STORIES YOU'LL NEVER FORGET
BY AUTHORS YOU'LL ALWAYS REMEMBER

The Editors

LOVESWEPT® • 238

Joan Elliott Pickart

Midsummer Sorcery

BANTAM BOOKS
TORONTO • NEW YORK • LONDON • SYDNEY • AUCKLAND

For Gen

MIDSUMMER SORCERY
A Bantam Book / February 1988

LOVESWEPT® and the wave device are registered trademarks of Bantam Books. Registered in U.S. Patent and Trademark Office and elsewhere.

If you would be interested in receiving protective vinyl covers for your Loveswept books, please write to this address for information:

Loveswept
Bantam Books
P.O. Box 985
Hicksville, NY 11802

ISBN 0-553-21869-7

Published simultaneously in the United States and Canada

Bantam Books are published by Bantam Books, a division of Bantam Doubleday Dell Publishing Group, Inc. Its trademark, consisting of the words "Bantam Books" and the portrayal of a rooster, is Registered in U.S. Patent and Trademark Office and in other countries. Marca Registrada. Bantam Books, 666 Fifth Avenue, New York, New York 10103.

PRINTED IN THE UNITED STATES OF AMERICA

O 0 9 8 7 6 5 4 3 2 1

One

"Fletcher McGill is back."

Nancy Forest stared at her seventeen-year-old brother, Kip. He sat across the table from her, giving serious attention to his huge lunch.

Nancy had the strange sensation of time having stopped. The earth stood still for a trembling moment, then tilted, dumping her off to land in the past with a shattering impact. Four little words had hurled her from thc hcre and now to the then, the days gone by: "Fletcher McGill is back."

Six years. It had been six years since—

"He can't walk," Kip said, then took a big bite of his sandwich.

"What?" Nancy whispered. She gripped the edge of the table as if it were a lifeline that would keep her from being flung into a dark sea of churning memories.

"Well, he can walk," Kip said, shrugging. "He's on

crutches, has a cast on his leg. He messed up his ankle pretty bad, I guess. Really creamed it. I was over there cutting the grass this morning, and they're all buzzing about it. Guess Fletcher just showed up in the middle of the night, and nobody knew he was coming."

"Did . . . did you see him?"

"Nope. He was sacked out. I heard Mrs. McGill talking to Shane while they were having breakfast on that fancy terrace of theirs. She sounded happy that Fletcher was home, I think, but I couldn't see the expression on her face. Shane mumbles, so I couldn't hear what he was saying. Why does a guy as old as Shane still live at home, anyway? What a mooch."

"That's old southern tradition, Kip. Some families still believe in several generations living under the same roof."

"Whatever. I gotta go," he said, getting to his feet. "Anyway, Fletcher McGill is back. 'Bye."

" 'Bye," Nancy said absently as Kip dashed out the door. A message of pain reached her brain, and she looked down to see that she was gripping the edge of the table so tightly that her knuckles were white. She pried her fingers free and clasped her hands in her lap, staring unseeing at a spot on the wall. "Fletcher . . . McGill . . . is . . . back."

As she spoke the words aloud, they seemed to fill the room, drawing the oxygen from it, making it difficult to breathe. Pictures, visions, images, from days gone by tumbled in her mind in a maze, twisting and turning, taunting. Fletcher's deep, rich voice reached out to her, repeating what she'd been unable to forget in six long years.

• • •

"You're beautiful, Nance. So beautiful. And you're mine. Understand?"

"Yes. Oh, yes, Fletcher, I'm yours. I love you so much. I've never been so happy."

"Come with me, Nance. We'll leave tonight after everyone is asleep."

"Fletcher, no. People will be hurt; your parents, my father."

"You're all I care about. Come with me. There's a whole world waiting for us out there."

"I need to think. I . . . Kiss me, Fletcher. Just kiss me, touch me. We'll talk about it later. Love me, Fletcher, here at our pond. Please."

Nancy blinked as the kitchen slowly came back into focus. Her eyes widened as she realized she'd pressed her fingertips to her lips, and she jerked her hands away, then stumbled to her feet.

"Damn you, Fletcher McGill," she said to the empty room. "Why did you have to come back? Why?"

Fletcher groaned as pain shot up his right leg. He shifted onto his back, noting that his cut-off jeans had left a film of dust on the velvet bedspread. He'd taken off his one shoe and his shirt, then quit, giving in to his fatigue and collapsing onto the bed. His mother and Shane had been hovering around, firing questions at him, but he'd been too exhausted to do more than mumble that he would see them in the morning.

Well, he thought dryly, he'd slept away the morning. The inquisition was now scheduled for afternoon. He needed to wash up, shave, have some food, then he'd face the mighty McGills. It would serve him right if they booted him out. A dozen or so postcards sent from all over the world in the past six years did not a dedicated son and brother make.

Six years, Fletcher mused. That was a helluva long time. He'd been twenty-four when he'd left; a young twenty-four, reckless, full of dreams, ready to take on the world, with all its challenges and adventures. He'd been restless, eager, bursting with energy, and consumed with love for Nancy Forest. His Nance.

He could see her so clearly, as though she were standing in the room with him. Her blue eyes would sparkle when she laughed, then turn smoky with desire as he took her into his arms. He'd adored her curls, so dark and bouncy, slipping through his fingers like threads of ebony silk. She was tiny, like a doll; she had made him feel strong and powerful. But he'd been gentle with her, always gentle, because he loved her with a sweet, aching pleasure that had made his blood run hot at the mere sight of her. She'd been part of his dreams and plans for the future.

"I can't do it, Fletcher. I can't sneak away in the night. It's wrong. Don't you understand that?"

"Shh, don't cry. Don't cry. Nance, this is the only way. I love you. I want you with me. You're eighteen. You can make your own decisions. I didn't draw the invisible line down the center of this town and say these are the rich, the worthy, and

those others are the inferior kind. I didn't do it, and I can't erase it. They'll hassle us so damn bad. The prejudice is on both sides of the line, too."

"I know."

"This is the only way, don't you see? Please, Nance, don't let them do this to us. Come with me."

"I can't! Oh, dear Lord, I'm scared. Your family has so much money. They'll find us; they'll—"

"No! We're both adults. We can do what we want. If you love me, really love me, you'll come."

"I do love you, but I can't do this. I can't, Fletcher."

"Dammit! I'll be here at the pond at two A.M. *If you're not here, I'm leaving without you. Do you hear me, Nancy? I'm leaving without you!"*

Fletcher ran his hand down his face and shook his head slightly, hoping to chase the tormenting scene from his mind. Nance hadn't come to the pond, and he'd gone away without her, filled with an immeasurable sense of betrayal.

Where was she now? he wondered. She'd be twenty-four years old. Was she married? Probably. Maybe had a baby or two. Lord, he hated the very thought of another man's hands on her small, firm breasts, touching her ivory skin, making love to her. He'd hated that image for six years. He had sought out women across the world, taken them to his bed in an attempt to dull the memories, but none of the women had had half the power of his Nance, and none could substitute in any way for her.

"Hell," he muttered. What was he doing here? Why

had he come back? He hadn't thought it through, just impulsively crawled home. He was damn tired, his ankle was smashed to smithereens, and for the life of him he didn't know why he was here. He didn't think or act like a McGill, never had, though heaven knew he'd given it his best shot for as long as he'd been able to stand it. He'd been twenty-four when the rebel within him had won, and he'd given up trying to please them, leaving in the middle of the night. Without Nance.

"Enough of this," he said, sitting up. He swung his uninjured leg over the side of the bed, then lifted the heavy cast that ended just below his knee, and lowered it gingerly to the floor. He'd spent too many hours on his feet the day before, he knew, and was paying the price now with bone-grinding pain. He'd have killed for a shower, but was sentenced to sponging off, or maneuvering into a bathtub with his leg elevated if there were someone around to help him. Well, it was sponge-bath detail today. For all he knew, everyone in this house would be only too happy if he drowned.

Fletcher reached down to the floor for his crutches and fitted them under his arms, leveling himself up with the next motion. He stared down at the duffel bag on the floor.

"Fly yourself into the bathroom, will ya?" he said to the dusty blue canvas bag. "Hell," he muttered again, and sank back onto the bed. He was clumsy and helpless and fuming mad at himself. He shouldn't have come home in this condition. Maybe he shouldn't have come home at all. Hell, he couldn't even walk down by the pond. The pond . . .

• • •

"I'm telling you, Nance, you're going to fall in."

"No, I'm not. This is an official ceremony. I hereby christen this secret place Fletcher's Pond, known only to Fletcher McGill and Nancy Forest."

"Hear, hear. Except that I doubt we're the only ones who know about it."

"Where's your sense of romance?"

"Come over here, sweet, sweet Nance, and I'll show you. Since I'm the Fletcher of the newly named Fletcher's Pond, I get to give the orders. Come here."

"Yes, sir. It will be my pleasure, sir."

"Our pleasure, Nancy mine. Ours. Together."

"Always, Fletcher."

Fletcher leaned down and unzipped the duffel bag. "Yeah, right," he said, a bitter edge to his voice. "Together. Always. Bull." One summer. That was all they'd had. One glorious, intense, in-love, making-love summer—the memories of which had haunted him for six long years.

Washed, shaved, and dressed in khaki shorts and a yellow knit shirt, Fletcher made his way slowly and carefully down the long, winding staircase. His mother, he assumed, was having lunch on the terrace. And his father? Fletcher had been so wiped out when he'd arrived, he hadn't asked where his father was. Well, he'd find out soon enough. He felt like a kid who had just been summoned to the principal's office. And with the remembrance of many of those command performances, he could feel the chip cn his shoulder beginning to take shape.

Easy, Fletch, he told himself. He was, after all, the

prodigal son returned. The members of his family had every right to tell him to haul his battered body right out the front door. It would be nice if they'd come to understand why he had gone, why he couldn't be another McGill popped out of the mold. But that was fantasy. What would take place was a twenty-question quiz as to where he'd been, what he'd been doing, and why he'd suddenly turned up unannounced. He had no intention of answering the first two questions, and the answer to the third was a mystery even to himself. This could very well be the longest lunch of his life.

"Fletcher," Elsie McGill said, getting quickly to her feet, "you should have called for help, dear. Shane, help your brother."

"No, I'm fine," Fletcher said, clumping his way across the terrace on his crutches. He bent and kissed his mother on the cheek, then lowered himself into a chair. He looked at his brother. "Hello, Shane. I suppose I said hello to you last night, but it's a bit of a blur."

"Fletch," Shane said, nodding. He definitely wasn't smiling.

Shane McGill was thirty-five, and had the same brown hair with blond highlights, the same dark brown eyes as his brother. There was a vague family resemblance in their features, but there the similarity stopped. Shane's hair was straight and cut short, compared to Fletcher's unruly waves, which grew thick over his ears and fell to the collar of his shirt. At six feet, Fletcher was taller, and he had a hard, lean, tightly muscled, tanned body. Shane was smaller-boned, with the beginning of a belly inching over his belt. There was more, Fletcher knew, than age and physical differences between him and his brother. They were worlds apart in terms of how they conducted their lives and what they considered important. They had simply never seen eye-to-eye on anything.

"Help yourself, dear," Elsie said to Fletcher. "You must be starved. Did you sleep well? I called your father. He's in Chicago on a business trip. He wondered . . . Well . . ."

"Wondered?" Fletcher repeated, reaching for a sandwich.

"How long you planned to stay."

"I'm not sure," Fletcher said. Shane made a noise that sounded distinctly like a snort of disgust. Fletcher ignored it. "I have to see a doctor in Atlanta about my ankle."

"Just what happened to it?" Shane asked.

"I broke it," Fletcher said, smiling pleasantly and revealing gleaming white teeth. "Smashed it up real good."

"That much we know," Shane said. "How did you break it?"

"I was in the wrong place at the wrong time. Is there coffee in that pot?"

"Of course," Elsie said, pouring him a cup. "I'll be happy to drive you into Atlanta whenever you need to go, Fletcher. Oh, I can't believe you're here. It's so wonderful to see you."

"Thanks, Mom."

"Where have you been for six years?" Shane asked.

Fletcher reached for another sandwich. "Didn't you get my postcards? I've been all over the world."

"Doing what?"

"You'd make a good cop, Shane," Fletcher said, looking directly at him. "Maybe you should have joined the FBI instead of working at McGill Textiles. By the way, how's business?"

"Since when do you care?" Shane asked.

"Shane, don't be rude," Elsie said. "We haven't seen Fletcher in six years. Don't begin our reunion by arguing."

"He has a point," Fletcher said. "The mill was never high on my list of interests. I was just making conversation."

"Do tell," Shane said. "Then why in the hell are you here?"

"Shane, stop it this instant," Elsie said.

"Right." Shane stood up. "I'll leave you to pamper your fair-haired boy, Mother. I'm due at the club for a golf game." He strode from the terrace.

"Enjoy," Fletcher said, reaching for yet another sandwich.

"I'm sorry, Fletcher," Elsie said. "Shane shouldn't have been so rude."

"I don't know about that, Mom. It seems to me you all have a right to feel any way you please about my absence." He covered his mother's hand with his. "Mom, listen to me, okay? I had to leave. Maybe taking off in the middle of the night wasn't the epitome of maturity, but at least it saved everyone from hearing Dad and me yell the roof down . . . again. I didn't belong here. I probably still don't."

"Oh, Fletcher," Elsie said, her eyes filling with tears.

"Hey, don't cry. Mom, you've always known I wasn't like Shane or Dad. I'm not cut out for a lifetime behind a desk at the mill."

"Yes," she said, reaching in her pocket for a linen handkerchief. "I knew. I never talked to you about it because . . . Oh, I don't know . . . I had some strange notion that if I acknowledged the fact that you didn't belong at the mill, if I encouraged you to discover where you really did belong, I'd be disloyal to your father. He was so determined that both you and Shane would take your rightful places in the business. Please, Fletcher, when he gets home don't provoke him. You both have the McGill temper, and you set each other off like a match put to dry grass."

"I'll be a nice boy," Fletcher said, and winked at her.

Elsie laughed and shook her head. "You scamp, you've always been too handsome for your own good. You've no doubt left a string of broken hearts around the world."

"Me?" Fletcher said, all innocence. "Don't be silly."

"Oh, I know better. There's something about you, a wild streak, an aura of the rebel, that suggests you can't be tamed. A woman adds it all up, along with your charm and good looks, and decides she's the one who will leash the beast."

Fletcher hooted with laughter. "Leash the beast? That's a unique way to put it. You will notice, ma'am, that I'm not leashed."

"No," Elsie said thoughtfully, "but I think you were once."

His smile instantly faded. "What?"

"There was something different about you the summer before you left. I can't define it; I just sensed a peacefulness, a gentle quality to you that hadn't been there before. I think you were in love that summer, Fletcher."

He shrugged, averting his gaze, then looking out over the perfectly manicured lawn beyond the terrace.

"You left her too," Elsie said quietly.

Fletcher's head snapped around, and anger flashed

in his dark eyes. "Not exactly. She wouldn't come with me. There's a big difference there."

"Who was she?"

"It's not important," he said tightly.

"It is if she's the reason you've come back."

"She isn't. I haven't been in contact with her since I left. I'm sure she's long gone from here. Probably she's married and has kids. Hell, I don't know. I don't care." Yes, he did. He did care, dammit.

"You care. I can see it in your eyes."

"Give it a rest, Mom. Please. It's over. It's been over for six years."

"What if she's still here in Oakville?"

"No," he said, shaking his head, "she wouldn't have stayed. Her plans were made until we—I'm sure she left soon after I did."

"Mrs. McGill," a uniformed woman said from the doorway, "Mrs. Winterson is on the phone. Shall I plug it in out here?"

"No, I'll come in. I need my notes on the charity ball. Fletcher, would you like Susie to bring you some peach pie?"

"No. No, thanks. Maybe later."

"All right, dear," Elsie said. She got to her feet and left the terrace.

Fletcher drew a deep breath and stared up at the clear blue April sky. No, he thought, Nance wasn't in Oakville, Georgia. She was in Atlanta, or New York, or someplace exciting. That was what she'd wanted before . . .

"Before I met you, Fletcher, all I could think about was getting out of Oakville. I'm enrolled in

business school in Atlanta for the fall, you know. But now—"

"Now?"

"Now I don't care where I go, as long as I'm with you. Maybe we'll spend the rest of our lives right here at Fletcher's Pond."

He chuckled. "Oh, okay. We'll live off cattails and pussy willows."

"We'll live," she whispered in a husky voice, "off love."

"I've created a monster."

"You've created a woman. Your *woman. I love you so much, Fletcher McGill."*

"And I love you, Nance. I never thought this would happen to me, but, Lord, how I do love you. I'm yours. I'm yours, Nancy."

Fletcher laughed, the sound hollow and empty. "She leashed the beast." He sighed. And the leash, he knew only too well, was still wrapped tightly around his heart.

Nancy spent the afternoon cleaning the house. It wasn't her usual Saturday dusting and vacuuming, but a frenzied scrubbing of windows, moving of furniture to get at the baseboards, straightening of cupboards that were already in perfect order. She pushed herself into a state of exhaustion with the fervent wish that when she fell into bed that night, she would be asleep in an instant.

It didn't work.

She lay staring up into the darkness for hours,

thinking about Fletcher McGill. The summer, that glorious, fairy-tale summer of six years ago, replayed over and over in her mind. Fletcher. So tall and bronzed, handsome beyond belief, wild and reckless, wonderful Fletcher. In their secret place, at Fletcher's Pond, he had taught her the ways of love, shown her the mysteries of his body and hers, watched her blossom into womanhood because of his gentle patience and knowing touch.

Oh, how she had loved him.

And, heaven help her, how she loved him still.

She'd learned, over the years, to push the memories away, to go weeks at a time without thinking of him, to look to the future and the day when she'd leave Oakville at last.

But now Fletcher was back, and with that knowledge the memories consumed her. It wasn't fair, she raged silently. She was so close to leaving; she was counting down the time in weeks. At last she was going to be free of the taunting remembrances of Oakville and Fletcher's Pond.

Why had he come? she wondered. Where had he been? How had his ankle been broken? Did he look different at thirty? Was he still reckless and full of energy, or had he settled down, grown serious like his father and brother? Had he brought a woman home with him? A wife? A lover? Oh, Lord, no. No! He loved *her*. He—No, that was six years ago. She'd had her chance to go with him, be with him, stay by his side. She'd been so young, so incredibly young and frightened, and she'd refused to go. And so he'd left her.

For weeks, day after day, she'd gone to Fletcher's Pond and waited for him. She'd been certain, so very certain, that he'd come back to her. But he hadn't come. She'd cried until she had no more tears left to shed, then gone to Atlanta to business school, moving in a strange, numb trance from one day to the next.

And now he was back.

And she still loved him.

And she hated him because she still loved him.

Tears burned her eyes, and her anger grew. She would *not* shed another tear for Fletcher McGill, for what might have been, for the memories of what they had had. It was as though that summer had been a dream; weeks, months, lifted out of reality in a rosy mist of first love. But the dream had ended. Life, with its sometimes harsh hand, had scattered the mist, brought facts and fears back into crystal clarity.

"Over," she said to the night. Of course it was over, for heaven's sake. She had been a child that summer, discovering love for the first time. The feelings she still had for Fletcher were suspended in a twilight zone, locked in the heart of an eighteen-year-old girl. She was a woman now, a woman who had faced tremendous adult responsibilities for the past six years. She was not the same person Fletcher had left behind at the pond.

Was it possible, she wondered, that if she saw Fletcher McGill at this very moment she would feel nothing? Would she be free at last from the ache in her heart for the man who had left her, left her to cry in confusion, pain, feeling so alone and betrayed?

It made sense, she thought, her heart racing. She had changed; surely Fletcher had changed. They were strangers. If she could see him, just once, without his seeing her, then probably she would discover that she really didn't love him anymore. Once that realization fell into place she could reclaim her heart as her own and move forward with her life.

Yes, she decided, that was what she would do. She would see Fletcher, somehow, and release herself from the hold he had on her.

"Fine," she said, and flopped over onto her stomach. Within moments, exhaustion claimed her and she slept.

Two

By the next Saturday morning, Nancy's nerves were stretched so tight that she imagined she would shoot straight up in the air, like a Fourth of July rocket, at the slightest provocation.

The week, on the surface, had been normal. Kip had gone to school each day, then worked afterward at the plant nursery. Nancy had gone to her cubbyhole office at Dr. Lansing's, doing the bookkeeping for the busy dentist.

From where she sat at her desk, she could see and hear the patients as June, the receptionist, greeted them. One topic, one juicy item, had taken front-row center all week as the patients came and went.

"Did you hear, June? That McGill boy is back. Fletcher, the troublemaker, you know the one. I wonder if he's hiding out from the law?"

"Do you remember Fletcher McGill, June? Well, he just showed up, nice as you please, without a howdy-do that he was coming. Glad I had girls. I'd have hated to raise a headstrong young man like that one."

"Bless my stars, Fletcher McGill is home. Elsie must be so happy. I remember that Fletcher when he was no bigger than a tadpole. He could charm me out of an extra cookie just by smiling. He's made of good stuff, that Fletcher. More to him than his father and brother put together."

"I heard, Miss June, that Fletcher McGill is awesome, just totally awesome. Do you think I look older than sixteen? I can't wait to see what he looks like, but I guess no one has seen him since he got back. But I did hear tell that he is awesome."

"Fletcher McGill. Yep. Fine boy. Reminds me of myself when I was young. Yep. He thinks for himself, don't let nobody shove him around. Yep. Fine boy."

And so it had gone through the week, with opinions of Fletcher offered free of charge until Nancy had been ready to scream. June had simply laughed at the hubbub that Fletcher was causing, and Nancy managed to reply with halfway-intelligent comments. It was apparent no one knew about that summer six years before, for Nancy had received no speculative glances, no inquiries as to whether she'd seen Fletcher. She'd simply smiled and gone about her usual business as the knot in her stomach twisted tighter and tighter. She had heard Fletcher's name over and over, but had no idea how she was going to get a glimpse of him.

Nancy looked out the window over the kitchen sink for the umpteenth time, then hurried to open the door.

"Kip," she said brightly, "I have your lunch all ready and waiting for you right there on the table. Wash up and dig in."

"Yes, ma'am." He patted her on top of the head.

"Don't do that. I hate that. You think you're so terrific because you shot up like a bean pole."

"This body got me a baseball scholarship to college, didn't it? Let's have a little respect for the junior member of this partnership." He washed his hands, then sat down at the table.

Nancy sat opposite him. "You know how proud I am of you, Kip," she said, smiling at him warmly. "And I'm so excited for you. Just think, the day after graduation you fly to California. You'll work on campus for the summer, then start college in the fall. You have your whole future ahead of you now."

"So do you. Finally. It's not fair that you had to come back after only three months in Atlanta to raise a bratty eleven-year-old brother."

"Hey, I'm crazy about that brother of mine." She smiled at him, then she added in a low, solemn voice, "Life isn't always fair, Kip. Our mother shouldn't have run off and left us all when you were just a baby. Dad worked hard at the mill and was in good health. He shouldn't have died of a heart attack. But I haven't been sitting around doing nothing for six years. You know I got hooked on computers during the three months I was in business school. I've done an analysis of nearly every business in Oakville, complete with full manual of instructions and what their computer needs are. Not that anyone went out and got computers, but the experience was wonderful. I have a very prestigious job at Cory Computer waiting for me in Atlanta, sir, thanks to pestering everyone in Oakville for all those years. The future is the important thing now."

"Yeah, you're right. I'm going to do a helluva job out in California, you'll see."

"Don't swear. I know you'll be great. I'm going to miss you. Help! Don't let me start on that or I'll cry. Eat your lunch." She waited several minutes as Kip took the edge off his appetite. "So! How did your morning go? Let's see, it's Saturday, so you were with the crew from the nursery, over at the McGills' house, right?"

"Yep."

"What's new there?" She hoped to high heaven that Kip couldn't hear the wild beating of her heart.

"Rose bushes."

Nancy groaned silently.

"Someday, Nancy, I'm going to get you a place that has a terrace like that. Do you know that the maid comes out and plugs in the phone so Mrs. McGill doesn't have to budge? Geez. I heard Mrs. McGill talking on the phone to Mr. McGill. She told him that she'd taken Fletcher into Atlanta to see the doctor. Do we have any potato chips?"

"No. Go on," she prompted. "Fletcher saw the doctor in Atlanta."

"Oh, yeah. Well, they changed his cast, put on one of those lightweight numbers that can get wet and stuff. He doesn't need crutches anymore, either. He moves around pretty good."

"You saw him?" Nancy asked, telling herself to remember to breathe.

"Yeah. He glanced over at me, but I'm sure he didn't recognize me. I was only eleven the last time I saw him. He looks"—he shrugged again—"I don't know."

She was going to strangle this kid! "How did he look, Kip?" she asked, striving for a casual tone.

"He's still got that shaggy hair, he's tan, he's . . ." Kip paused. "It's hard to explain. He's got a great build, wide shoulders, tight muscles, an athlete's body. He moves smoothly even with the cast. I knew Fletcher pretty well once, you know, because he helped out with the Little League. Well, today when he glanced over at me there was a difference in him."

"What do you mean?"

"His eyes. They're cold. There's just something cold, creepy, about his eyes. I guess this sounds dumb."

"No," Nancy said softly, "it doesn't. Fletcher's emotions used to be mirrored in his eyes."

"How do you know about his eyes?"

"What? Oh, I . . . Well, everyone knows everyone in Oakville, Kip. I met Fletcher at one of your Little League games, remember? We talked . . . in the past.

I just happen to remember that he has very expressive eyes."

"Ice cubes."

"I wonder what has caused his eyes to become so cold?"

"Who knows? Six years is a long time. No telling what he's been doing. He used to be my hero, you know what I mean? He was always laughing, messing around, and he was good at every sport he tried. I was going to call out to him today, tell him who I was, but then I saw his eyes, saw the way he seemed to look right through me. I figured, 'Forget this. I'll pass.' I think he's really changed, Nancy. Maybe I'm wrong but—I gotta go. I'm due back at work."

" 'Bye, Kip," she said as he ran out the door. She got slowly to her feet and began to clear the table, Kips words echoing in her mind.

Fletcher's eyes, she mused. They were so cold that a seventeen-year-old boy had noticed? A boy who had been a mere child the last time he'd looked into those eyes? What had happened to Fletcher in the past six years? She remembered his eyes—so brown. They'd danced with laughter, flashed with anger, grown soft and smoky when he'd taken her in his arms.

Eyes, the poets said, were the window to a man's soul. Had Fletcher changed so much that he was cold within himself?

Who was this Fletcher McGill who had come home?

A strange restlessness gripped Nancy on Sunday afternoon. It was different from the jangled state of her nerves she'd been suffering from all week. It was a sense of waiting, an anticipation of something about to happen. Yet she had no idea what it was.

The house was quiet, too quiet, as Kip was off to his usual Sunday baseball game in the park. Nancy wandered into her bedroom and stood in front of the full-length mirror that hung on her closet door.

Suppose, she mused, just suppose that Fletcher caught a glimpse of *her* while he was in Oakville. What would he see? How would she compare to the eighteen-year-old Nance he had loved that summer so long ago? Not that it mattered, not that she cared, but had she aged well?

She leaned closer to the mirror and peered at herself. For Pete's sake, she thought with disgust, she still looked eighteen. Her breasts were no bigger, her hips hadn't blossomed into voluptuous curves, freckles still dotted her nose. Her naturally curly hair was longer. . . . Oh, big deal. It tumbled to her shoulders now, but beyond that? There she stood, as she always had, cute little Nancy Forest in her jeans and cotton blouse.

"Yuk," she said, making a face at herself. Fletcher had traveled the world, had no doubt kept company with women of sophistication and glamour. They'd probably worn slinky sequined gowns and called everyone "dah-ling." Fletcher could pick from the crème de la crème to wine, dine, and bed. Took them to bed? All those women? What a rotten man!

Nancy sank to the edge of her bed with a sigh. She had no right to stand in judgment of Fletcher. Whether he'd been a bed-hopper or a candidate for the priesthood was none of her business. When she'd stood by the edge of Fletcher's Pond and told him she couldn't, wouldn't, go with him, she'd given up her place in his life.

Fletcher's Pond, she mused. She hadn't been near it in years. After her father had died and she'd returned to Oakville, she'd sought solace by the pond. She'd cried for her father, for Kip, for herself, for her shattered dreams and plans. And she'd cried because she needed Fletcher to be with her, to comfort her, to soothe her sorrow and her fears. She'd been so young and alone, facing the responsibility of raising a boy.

But Fletcher had been gone, so she'd squared her shoulders and carried on. Her aptitude for math had gotten her the job with Dr. Lansing, she'd continued to make the mortgage payments on the small house she'd grown up in, and she'd been a good sister and mother substitute to Kip. She dated various young men, was active in several civic groups, had worked hard at gaining her computer knowledge, and dreamed of the day when she could leave Oakville forever.

Nancy got to her feet and began to pace the floor. She was close, so close, to her goal. The house was up for sale, Kip's future was secure, and there were only weeks left until he graduated. Then *she* would leave Oakville far, far behind.

Fletcher's Pond, she thought, stopping her trek back and forth. She would go there, after all these years, see it for what it was; a secluded little pond nestled in the woods at the edge of town. It was simply water and pussy willows, cattails and trees. It wasn't a magical place of ecstasy created only for her and Fletcher.

It was time, she decided, to put Fletcher's Pond in

its proper perspective. That would be her first step. Then, somehow, she'd see Fletcher, even if she had to hide in the bushes on the McGill estate. And that would be step two, the final step. She'd be free.

In a sudden burst of energy, Nancy ran from the room and out the back door of the house. She was going to Fletcher's Pond!

Memories. Dear heaven, the memories.

Nancy's heart was racing as she stepped through the trees and saw the shimmering water of the little pond. Unable to stop herself, feeling like a marionette whose strings were being pulled by an invisible hand, she walked to the plush grass where she and Fletcher had first become lovers. Dreams had been woven here, secrets shared, fantasies spun. Here she had become a woman, giving herself totally, joyously, to the only man she had ever loved.

Nancy sank to the ground and pulled her knees up, wrapping her arms around her trembling legs. It was rushing back over her, all of it, replaying in her mind like an exquisite movie known only to her and Fletcher. No, she thought, Fletcher had probably long since forgotten this pond, her, that summer. The memories were hers alone, and she didn't want them. She would be strong and crush them into dust, then scatter them into the wind and oblivion. She was Nance Forest, and she would—No! She was Nancy. Only Fletcher had . . .

"Nance, look, there's a cardinal in that tree."

"Nance," she said, laughing softly. "You're the only one who calls me that."

"I know. It's a special name for my special girl. I don't want anyone using that name but me."

"My, my, how possessive," she said teasingly.

"Damn right. You're mine. You'll always be mine. You are my Nance, Nance, Nance . . ."

"Nance?"

Nancy blinked and stiffened as she stared out over the water. It was as though Fletcher had spoken, had said her name in that rich, deep, beautiful voice of his. Maybe she shouldn't have come here. Maybe the memories were too strong.

"Nance? Is it really you? No, I'm imagining this. Aren't I? Nancy?"

She turned her head, hardly breathing.

And there he was.

Fletcher McGill.

Magnificent Fletcher, she thought hazily. So tall, tanned, handsome. He looked shocked, as though he'd seen a ghost. Had his shoulders always been that wide, his arms and legs so corded with muscles? He was wearing navy blue shorts and a white knit shirt. The cast. Yes, there it was, just as Kip had said. His eyes. She had to look at his eyes to see if they had grown cold, hard, giving a glimpse into his soul and who he had become.

He moved slowly forward to stand beside her, towering over her. "Nance? Say something, anything. Give me some clue that I'm not dreaming this."

Nancy swallowed. "Hello, Fletcher."

"Lord, it *is* you," he said, shaking his head slightly.

"I can't believe this." He lowered himself to the grass next to her, easing his injured leg into a comfortable position. His gaze swept over every inch of her and settled at last on her blue eyes.

Neither spoke.

They simply looked into each other's eyes for a timeless moment . . . and remembered.

Fletcher's eyes weren't cold, Nancy thought dreamily. They were the same warm brown. No, now there was a flicker of something else. Anger. Yes, there it was. He was angry. At her? Why? He was the one who had left. He was the one who hadn't written or called in six years, just dusted her off as a silly summer romance. And *he* was angry?

She turned and stared at the pond as she tightened her arms around her drawn-up knees. She heard Fletcher take in a deep breath and let it out slowly.

"I didn't know you were in Oakville," he said, his voice low. "Are you visiting your father and Kip?"

"My father is dead," she said softly, still not looking at him.

"He's—When? When did he die?"

"In the fall, after Thanksgiving, that year that you . . . that you left."

"Lord, I'm sorry. I didn't know. What about Kip? Who took care of him?"

"I did. I came home from Atlanta and raised him."

"Oh, damn," Fletcher said, running his hand down his face. "Are you saying you've been here in Oakville for the past six years? You never had a chance to follow your own dreams, make a life for yourself?" He took a deep breath. "Or . . . or did you? Did you marry someone here?"

She shook her head.

"Oh." Fletcher's mind was racing. This was unbelievable. All these years she'd been right here in Oakville. She'd been raising her brother. She hadn't been occupying another man's bed and having his babies, as he'd tortured himself into believing. And she looked the same. She was beautiful. Her hair was longer, but other than that she was Nance, his Nance, sitting there in their special place at Fletcher's Pond and—No! Dammit, he had to get a grip on himself. Six years had passed since they'd been lovers in this grass. He didn't know her, not really. Hell, yes, he did. He knew her; he loved her; he'd never stopped loving her. And he wanted her. "Nance, I—"

"Nancy," she said, snapping her head around to look at him. "My name is Nancy. Nance was an eighteen-year-old child who doesn't exist anymore." His lips. She remembered those lips, how they felt moving over hers. Soft, wonderful lips. "I'm Nancy."

"Not to me. You were Nance then, and you're Nance now. Why are you here?"

"I told you."

"No, I don't mean, why are you in Oakville? Why are you here at Fletcher's Pond, in this spot, our special place? I came to relive the memories, to think about you. Why did *you* come?"

"To relive the memories so that I could forget about you," she said sharply. "I'm leaving Oakville in a few weeks, when Kip graduates. I'm leaving and never coming back. And when I go, I'll be free of the past, of the memories, of you. I saw it, Fletcher. I saw the anger in your eyes when you looked at me. You still can't believe it, can you? You can't believe that

Fletcher McGill didn't get his own way six years ago."

"You should have come with me," he said, his voice rising.

"You should have come back to me! You went off in a huff, and that was that. I was young, so young and frightened and . . . But all you could think about was what *you* wanted." His hands. So strong, but so very gentle. They'd always looked dark against her pale skin. His hands. On her breasts. Moving lower, then lower yet. Making her burn with the need, the want, of him. "Forget it. Just forget it. There's no point in discussing any of this. We had a summer fling. That's it. People do it all the time."

Fletcher's hands shot out and gripped her upper arms. "Dammit, don't say that. Don't make it sound cheap, sordid, because it wasn't." And because he still loved her, and what they'd had that long-ago summer was precious and rare and beautiful. "Don't tarnish it, Nance."

"My God," she whispered, "it's true, just as Kip said. Your eyes have turned cold. I've never seen your eyes like that, Fletcher. What has happened to you?"

"Dammit," he said, giving her a small shake, "would you forget about my eyes? Listen to me, Nance, please."

"There's nothing to say, nothing to discuss or rehash," she said, lifting her chin. His hands caused heat to travel up her arms and across her breasts. Her breasts began to ache for his touch, the gentle pull of his mouth on her soft flesh. Oh, dear heaven, it was all there—the desire, the want and need for this man. Six years had dimmed nothing. And, oh, damn, she thought, with every breath in her body, every beat of her heart, she still loved him. "No," she said, shaking her head. "Oh, no, no, no."

"Nance," he said, his tone softening. He eased his hold on her arms, but didn't release her. "I was so hurt, just totally blown away when you wouldn't come with me, I didn't know what to do with all those emotions, so I turned them into anger. I went as far as I could, as fast as I could, trying to outrun my pain. But you were with me, in my heart, in my mind, every inch of the way."

"Six years, Fletcher," she murmured. "Not one word from you in six years."

"I thought you were gone. I tortured myself with images of you, finding someone else, getting married, having that man's baby. Oh, Nance, if I had known about your father, about your being left alone to raise Kip, I would have come back to you. I swear it."

"It doesn't matter now," she said, her voice flat.

"Yes, it does. Everything matters. You, me, us together. This is our special place. This is Fletcher's Pond. Think about what we shared here. Think about the first time we made love, and all the times after that. Oh, yes, it matters, all of it."

"Good Lord, Fletcher, do you think you can just waltz in here after six years and pick up where you left off? We're here at Fletcher's Pond, so why not have a little tumble in the grass? I'm not the naive, dewy-eyed child I was then. I've grown up and grown wiser. When I leave Oakville in a few weeks, I'm not taking any memories of you with me. I'll be free, Fletcher McGill."

"Are you so very sure of that?" he asked in a low voice. "Are you, Nance?"

"Yes."

"Can you forget this?" he asked, and brought his mouth down hard onto hers.

No, don't! Nancy screamed silently. She had dreamed of this kiss, ached for this kiss, waited six long years for this kiss. She mustn't respond to him, mustn't let him know she still loved him. He'd only leave her again, hurt her again. This was reckless, restless Fletcher, who would seek out the next adventure, the untried road, simply because it was there. She wasn't going through heartbreak again. No!

The punishing onslaught of Fletcher's mouth gentled. He wove his fingers into her hair to hold her head steady as she pushed futilely against the unyielding wall of his chest. His tongue slid insistently over her lips and Nancy felt the hot curl of desire deep within her spread, bursting into a flame that licked through her entire body.

She parted her lips and received Fletcher's tongue into her mouth, a soft sob catching in her throat. Of their own volition, it seemed, her hands moved up his chest to circle his neck, her fingers inching into his thick, wavy hair.

Fletcher's hands dropped to her back; roaming, warm, strong hands that ignited her passion further. He lowered her to the plush grass, his lips never leaving hers as he partially covered her body with his. He lifted his head only long enough to draw air into his lungs, then claimed her mouth again, thrusting his tongue deep within. He ached to become one with his love, his only love.

He'd found his Nance, he thought hazily, and he'd never lose her, never leave her again.

"Oh, Nance," he murmured close to her lips, "I want you so much. I never stopped loving you. You're mine. You've always been mine."

Fletcher's words sifted through the rosy mist of passion clouding Nancy's mind. She didn't want to hear, she only wanted to feel. Fletcher was there, tasting so good, smelling so good, bringing back such glorious memories. She wanted him. She loved him. He was home.

"You're mine. Let me love you, Nance, here. Here, at Fletcher's Pond."

No, her mind whispered, then gained force, shouting at her to listen, really listen, to what he was saying.

"No," she said, pushing against his chest. "I'm not yours. Not anymore. Not ever again. I'm leaving, don't you understand? I don't want this. I don't want *you*, Fletcher McGill."

She saw the flicker of pain in his dark eyes and felt as though a cold hand had clutched her heart. She had to do it this way, she told herself frantically. She couldn't get caught up in the sensual web he was capable of weaving around her. She was going to walk away from him and not look back.

Fletcher shifted off her and sat up, drawing a deep breath into his lungs as he raked his hand through his hair. Nancy struggled to sit up, willing her heart to return to a normal rhythm.

"I don't believe you," Fletcher said, staring out over the water. His voice was low and husky. "You *do* want me. You responded to me totally, just the way you did six years ago."

"I won't deny that you know how to arouse me," she said coolly. "After all, you're the one who taught me all about sex."

"Not sex," he said sharply, jerking his head around to look at her. "Making love. There's a helluva difference there, and you know it. Sex is what I've had for the past six years. *You* are the only woman I've ever made love with."

"Semantics." She plucked a blade of grass and studied it intently. She couldn't handle this much longer, she thought with a rush of panic. She was a breath away from bursting into tears, throwing herself into Fletcher's arms, telling him she'd never stopped loving him, missing him. What he had just said about her being the only woman he'd ever made love with was so beautiful. She'd been with no man since Fletcher. She'd dated, kissed her escorts good night at the door, and that was it. There'd been only Fletcher. She had to get away from him, away from Fletcher's Pond, before it all came tumbling out in a jumble of words. "I'm going home," she said, starting to stand.

He grabbed her arm. "The hell you are. We're not finished here."

She met his gaze. "Yes, we are, Fletcher. We were finished six years ago. I don't know where you've been or why you've suddenly come back, and I don't care. May I have my arm, please?"

He stared at her for a long moment, and Nancy willed herself to look directly at him with no readable expression on her face. He slowly lifted his hand from her arm.

Now came the tricky part, Nancy thought dryly. She had to make a dignified exit on legs that felt like spaghetti. She had to leave with her head held high and pray to the heavens that she didn't cry until she was safely home.

She got to her feet and brushed off the seat of her pants. "Good-bye, Fletcher." He didn't speak as she turned and started away.

"Nance."

She stopped, her back to him. "Yes?"

"I'll see you soon," he said, his voice low.

"No."

"Very, very soon."

"No," she whispered, then hurried away.

Fletcher watched her cross the grass, then disappear into the woods. He felt an aching loss when he could no longer see her, then placed his hand on the grass beside him to feel the warmth still lingering there from her body.

"Ah, Nance," he said, with a moan, "I love you so damn much." All those years, he thought incredulously, she'd been here, right here in Oakville. The times that he'd considered coming home he'd pictured only an emptiness waiting for him because she'd be gone. So he hadn't come. He was only home now because of an impulsive action. He hadn't analyzed it or thought it through. He'd simply gotten on a plane and come home.

Fletcher stretched out on his back and laced his hands under his head, staring up at the sky as the warm sun washed over him. How strange it all was, he mused. If he'd delayed, talked himself out of getting on that plane, waited until another time, Nancy would have been gone. At least now he knew what he was doing here, why he'd suddenly found himself back in Oakville. He'd come for his Nance, his love, his life.

But how did Nance feel, really feel, about him? She'd responded to his kiss totally, and it was not, by damn, simply because he knew how to arouse her. What a crummy thing for her to say. Oh, she'd tried to come across as a tough little cookie, who didn't give a damn if he took a flying leap, but he'd heard the trembling in her voice, seen the soft, smoky hue of desire in her blue eyes.

Okay, he admitted, maybe she wasn't in love with him anymore, but she cared, felt something for him. He'd take any points he could get. She was hurt and defensive, and had walls as solid as concrete built around her. But she *did* care about him, he'd make book on it. Oh, Lord, she had to!

She could have asked him about his ankle, he thought. Didn't it bother her that he was among the walking wounded? Didn't a cast call for a little sympathy? His mother had flipped out when she'd seen the condition he was in. But Nance? She hadn't even made a polite inquiry. Brother.

Fletcher swatted a fly away, then put his hand back under his head. Where, he wondered, had all his anger disappeared to? Almost from the moment he had seen Nancy, the fury that had built up within him over the years had dissolved and been replaced by the warm glow of knowing he loved the woman before him. The emotions of the summer six years before had swamped him and he'd felt renewed, whole again. He liked being in love, but it would help immensely if the person he loved returned those feelings in kind.

Well, he thought, she'd loved him once; she'd love

him again, pure and simple. Maybe it wasn't going to be simple, but it *was* going to happen. He loved her and wanted her, but even more, he needed her. He was so damn tired of moving through life alone. He'd accomplished what he'd set out to do, and now he wished for someone to share it with. But it had to be Nance. And it would be. He was going to win her back. Somehow.

"She could have asked about my ankle, for Pete's sake," he said, then yawned. Just before he drifted off to sleep, he begrudgingly admitted to himself that he was pouting.

Nancy hardly remembered getting home. The next thing she was totally aware of was flinging herself across her bed and giving way to her tears. Her tears, she realized, were not from sorrow, but from anger, frustration, and a niggling sense of fear.

She was furious at herself for succumbing to the magic of Fletcher's kiss. She raged in anger at herself to think that after all these years, after Fletcher had gone off and left her, she still loved him with the same intensity as before.

And she was scared to death that her love for him and his sexual power over her would somehow trap her, hold her in Oakville for as long as he chose to stay.

She rolled over onto her back and stared up at the ceiling, dashing the unwelcome tears from her cheeks. No way, Fletcher McGill, she fumed. He wasn't doing this to her again. With any luck, he'd pack up and be gone the next day.

Gone? her mind echoed. After swooping into town,

kissing her senseless, stirring up old desires and dreams, he'd just saunter off and disappear? The gall, the nerve of the man. How could he do this?

"Oh-h-h," she moaned, "I'm losing my mind." She was! She was slipping over the edge. She was angry that he'd come back, and furious that he'd consider leaving just as quickly. As Kip would say, her ducks were not lined up in a straight row.

She had to calm down, she told herself firmly. Was she a flaky eighteen-year-old kid? No, she was not. Was she a mature woman capable of making her own decisions, choosing her own destiny? Yes, she was. Did she melt like butter in the sun when Fletcher touched and kissed her? Erase that. She refused to answer. She wouldn't think about it.

So, okay, she admitted, her plan to see Fletcher and realize that he no longer meant anything to her had fizzled. Brother, had it ever. She loved him, the louse, and she might as well accept that fact. But he didn't know that she loved him, and that was definitely in her favor!

There he had sat at Fletcher's Pond, she mused, declaring his love for her. He'd never stopped loving her, he'd said, had missed her and tortured himself with the image of her belonging to another man. The words had flowed from his luscious lips like honey: sweet and warm, spoken in a voice thick with passion, husky with sensuality.

And she didn't believe a damn word of what he had said!

No sirreebob, she wasn't falling for that malarkey. She didn't know why he had come home. That he was already getting restless and bored, she could well imagine. He must have felt as though he'd won the lottery when he'd found good old, gullible Nance by the pond. Things in Oakville, Mr. McGill had probably decided, might not be so dull after all. He would occupy his time picking up where he'd left off with Nancy Forest six years before.

Over her dead body!

Bad choice of words, Nancy instantly thought. She wouldn't think about Fletcher's being over her body, touching her body, entering her body with power tempered with gentleness—No, cancel all thoughts of bodies.

"Just shut up, Nancy," she said to herself, feeling the warm flush on her cheeks. Plan A with steps one and two was a dud. She had to regroup and start over. She would, she supposed, have to accept the fact that she was still deeply in love with Fletcher, and know that when she left Oakville the image of Fletcher, the memories of Fletcher, the very essence of Fletcher, would go with her.

So be it, she thought. She didn't like it, but there didn't seem to be much she could do about it. The important thing now was to stay away from Fletcher McGill! She was in rough enough shape without adding to the damage by seeing him, hearing his laughter, or, heaven forbid, melting into his arms.

Her performance at the pond, she concluded, had been superb. Well, she'd have to deduct points for kissing him, but other than that, she'd put on quite a show. She'd made it very clear that it was over between them, had been for years, and she simply wasn't interested in him anymore. She, who had been raised not to lie, had rattled off a string of beauts. Fletcher could find other pastures to plow—or however that went—while he was in town. Fine. Yes, fine and dandy, as long as she didn't go within twenty feet of him. Surely she could manage that if she kept alert. If he left soon, she'd be home free. If not, she had only a few weeks to make certain that she stayed out of his way.

Nancy stood, then plopped back down on the edge of the bed. His eyes, she thought suddenly. Fletcher's eyes. They'd been warm, just as she'd remembered them. Then she'd seen the cold curtain drop, the one that had impressed Kip. Wherever Fletcher had been, whatever he'd seen and done, had taken a toll. He'd been a young and, yes, somewhat immature twenty-four when he'd left Oakville. Now, it seemed, he was older than his years. He'd grown up to and beyond thirty years of age. Oh, not physically. He was beautiful with his added maturity, absolutely magnificent. No, it was something within him—a layer of steel, perhaps, a hardness that showed itself in the chilling change that came over his eyes.

Nancy shivered, then stood again. She glanced at the clock, realized that it was time to start dinner, and went into the bathroom to splash water on her face. She was going out to the movies that night with handsome Brad Sanders, who worked in the bank. Good. It would take her mind off Fletcher. She hoped.

The movie was the most ridiculous thing Nancy had ever seen. She didn't care how powerful the potion was that the Russians had developed, it couldn't have produced an ant large enough to gobble up New York City in a dozen bites. Really dumb.

"Dumb, dumb, dumb," she said.

Brad laughed. "Hey, that was a terrific ant. I love those flicks. Look, there's Sissie and Bill. Want to have some ice cream with them?"

"Sure," Nancy said.

The ice cream parlor had old-fashioned wrought-iron tables and chairs, with bright tablecloths and matching pillows tied onto the chair seats. It was the place to go following social outings in Oakville, and as always a chattering crowd was filing in after the movie. The four found a table, and a very pregnant Sissie eased herself down into a chair with a sigh.

"That poor ant," Sissie said. "The Marines blasted him into a zillion pieces."

"She's going to cry now," Bill said calmly to Nancy and Brad. "It's really amazing what sets her off."

"I want ice cream," Nancy said. "I can't handle one more thought about that awful ant. If I dream about him tonight, I'll sue."

"Speaking of dreams," Sissie said. "When I was in high school I spent hours daydreaming about that hunk who just came in the door."

"Who?" Bill asked, grinning. "I'll kill the bum. Hey! It's Fletch. You had a crush on Fletcher McGill?"

"The whole female population did," Sissie said. "Well, not you, Nancy, I guess. You're younger than we are."

Would they notice, Nancy thought frantically, if she crawled under the table? Oh, Lord, Fletcher was here, and she'd give anything not to be.

Bill got to his feet. "Fletch!" he yelled. "Quit playing ambassador and talking to everyone. Get your backside over here, you old reprobate."

Father-to-be or not, Nancy fumed, she was going

to sic the ant on Bill. Oh, how could he do this to her? And look; now Brad was on his feet, waving Fletcher over. Fletcher was smiling and nodding and walking their way. And he was gorgeous. Red T-shirt and faded tight, tight jeans, slit up one leg to accommodate the cast. He was getting closer and closer and . . .

"Hey!" Bill said, flinging his arms around Fletcher. "Damn, it's good to see you, Fletch."

"It sure is good to see you, too," Fletcher said. "How are you? Hey, Brad, you're looking great." He shook Brad's hand. "Hi, Sissie. You're even more beautiful than I remember. I think pregnant women are exquisite."

"Oh-h-h," Sissie said, sniffling into her napkin.

Fletcher shifted his gaze to Nancy. "Hello, Nancy. Enjoy the movie?"

"She hated it," Brad said. "I don't know why. I only take her to state-of-the-art stuff. Grab a chair, Fletch, and join us. This brings back memories. Here we are, the three stars of the Oakville High School football team, together again."

Fletcher chuckled, and commandeered a chair from another table. There was a shifting and shuffling as everyone made room for him, and Nancy watched in wide-eyed horror as he slid his chair between hers and Sissie's.

"Figures," Bill said, laughing. "Leave it to Fletch to make sure he's close to the pretty women."

"Damn right," Fletcher said. "I'm no fool."

His thigh, Nancy thought, fuming, was pressed against hers. His warm, muscled thigh, and she didn't have one inch of room to move away.

"Well, Fletcher," Brad said, "you've got the whole

town buzzing, as usual. You're the only guy I know who can cause a stir just by showing up."

"Six years is a long time," Sissie said. "Rumor has it that you've been all over the world."

"Yep," Fletcher said, nodding.

"Is there a big secret about why you've suddenly come home?" Brad asked.

"Not really," Fletcher said. He ran his hand lightly along Nancy's thigh to her knee. She stiffened in her chair. He continued to look directly at Brad. "I just have some unfinished business here."

Three

Fletcher McGill, Nancy decided fiercely, was not worth going to jail for. But, oh, for two cents she'd murder him, drown him in his ice cream, hire the giant ant to gobble him up.

He refused, absolutely refused, to move his hand!

His big, strong, warm hand, which she was sure was scorching her white slacks from the heat it was generating. Heat that was traveling up and around and through her. Heat that was causing an ache deep within her. Heat that was bringing a flush to her cheeks and a flutter to her pulse.

She'd poked and pushed at his hand, tried to pry his fingers loose, managed to sneak her spoon under the table to render a solid whack to his knuckles, but the hand remained firmly in place.

Fletcher was taking part in a conversation centered on football days at Oakville High, his expression pleasant, his voice light. Nancy refused to look at him while she ate her ice cream.

Unfinished business in Oakville, huh? she thought. She'd finish his business when she cheerfully shot him! How dare he sit there and maul her under the table? Well, he wasn't exactly mauling her. It was only one hand on one knee, but it still took a lot of gall, she raged silently. She was, after all, out with Brad Sanders. It wasn't socially acceptable behavior to plunk one's big, strong, warm hand on the knee of another man's date. Didn't Fletcher have any couth?

Nancy glanced around the table and realized that no one had any idea of the war between the hand and the knee that was taking place. And none of these people, whom she'd known all of her life, knew that she and Fletcher had been lovers six years before. They were all just chatting away, totally oblivious to the currents of tension and sexuality crackling between her and Fletcher.

If they only knew, Nancy thought, swallowing a sudden bubble of laughter. How the affair between her and Fletcher had gone undetected six years ago, she'd never know. It was amazing, since in Oakville it was common for eight people to say, "bless you," when someone sneezed. Everyone knew everyone else's business.

She and Fletcher had been supersneaks, she thought merrily. They had pulled off the coup of the decade at Fletcher's Pond. The city mothers and fathers would gasp in horror if they knew what had taken place in that plush, fragrant grass. Oh, Lord, how funny. Why it was so funny, she wasn't exactly sure, but it just suddenly seemed extremely funny.

And so she laughed.

It was unfortunate that the topic of conversation

at the time was the bill before the city council regarding the legality of raising chickens within the city limits. Sissie, who raised chickens, was passionately defending her right to supplement her income by selling eggs, when Nancy cut loose with peals of laughter.

Everyone at the table stopped talking.

Everyone at the table stared at Nancy.

Fletcher slowly removed his hand from Nancy's knee and eyed her warily.

Nancy attempted to speak, shook her head, and continued to laugh. She wrapped her arms around her stomach and gasped for breath.

Fletcher reached over and whacked her on the back.

"Oh!" she said.

He grinned at her. "You're supposed to say, 'Thanks, I needed that.' What is your problem?"

"Problem?" she repeated, glancing quickly around the table. "There's no problem."

"I don't think my chickens are funny," Sissie said, looking as though she were about to cry again. "I adore my chickens, and they make cute little eggs, and—"

"They're very nice chickens, honey," Bill said, squeezing her hand. "Nancy wasn't laughing at your chickens."

"No, no, of course I wasn't," Nancy said. "I think your chickens are just superduper. Really! I was laughing at . . ." She searched her mind frantically for something to say.

"At?" Fletcher asked, leaning toward her.

She glared at him. "The ant. The stupid ant in the movie. I suddenly thought about the ant and . . .

Well, it was funny. Not hysterical, but . . . Oh, forget it."

Brad laughed. "I bet you do dream about that ant tonight, Nancy. If it crept up on you in the middle of a conversation about chickens, you'll dream about it for sure."

"Not if she concentrates on something else," Fletcher said, his hand sliding back into place on her knee. Nancy jumped in her chair. "Something pleasant, familiar, something associated with nice, warm, satisfying feelings."

"Like ice cream," Sissie said, and took a big bite of her banana split.

"Concentrate, Nancy," Fletcher said, in a low, husky voice, "on something nice and warm and, oh, so satisfying."

She turned her head to look at him, and discovered he'd leaned so close to her, she nearly bumped his nose. His eyes were looking directly into hers. She couldn't move, could hardly breathe, as the room disappeared into a hazy mist.

"How'd you break your ankle, Fletch?" Bill asked.

"What?" Fletcher slowly dragged his gaze from Nancy's. She turned and stared into her ice cream dish, her heart racing.

"Your ankle. How did you break it?"

"Oh, I jumped out of a moving Jeep and landed on a big rock that had the nerve to be in the way." He shrugged. "It was just one of those things that happen."

"Why would you jump out of a moving Jeep?" Nancy asked, looking at him again.

"Because it was about to go over a cliff," he said. Damn. He'd been sidestepping the question about his ankle just fine until now. Until he'd nearly drowned in Nancy's beautiful blue eyes. Until the blood was pounding so hot in his veins, he couldn't think straight, and he'd turned into a motor mouth. "It's not all that interesting a story."

"Oh, right," Brad said dryly, "it's very dull. Good Lord, man, what have you been doing for the past six years?"

"Brad, shh," Sissie said in a loud whisper. "Maybe Fletcher is a secret agent for our government and he's not allowed to tell us. Fletcher, are you a secret agent?"

"No," he said laughing. "I'm definitely not a secret agent. I just traveled around, that's all. The Jeep bit was an accident, nothing fancy."

"You traveled around," Bill repeated. "Doing what?"

"This and that. I'll tell you all about it someday." He'd tell everyone when he was ready, when the time was right. But he wanted to tell Nance first. If she wanted to hear. If she came to love him again.

"I imagine you've got some great stories to tell," Brad said, smiling. "You always knew where the fun and action were, Fletch."

"Yeah," Fletcher said quietly.

Nancy looked at him quickly. Cold, she thought. His eyes were ice cold. He was thinking about some thing or things he'd done or seen or—Dear heaven, where had he been? What had he really been doing? And why?

"Well, little mama," Bill said, "it's time to get you home and tucked into bed. It was great seeing you, Fletch. Are you going to stick around Oakville a while?"

Fletcher shrugged. "Depends." He got to his feet

and shook Bill's hand, then kissed Sissie on the cheek. "Take care of that baby, beautiful."

Depends? Nancy mentally repeated. What kind of an answer was that? His "unfinished business" and his articulate "depends" had better not have anything to do with her. They'd just better not!

"We should hit the road, too, Nancy," Brad said. "Monday mornings come all too early."

"Right," she said, jumping to her feet. "Let's go. 'Bye, Sissie. 'Bye, Bill. 'Bye, Fletcher. Come on, Brad." She grabbed his arm.

"We have to settle the bill," Brad said.

"Oh," she said, releasing his arm. She pursed her lips together as she heard Fletcher's low, sexy chuckle behind her.

Outside, the group parted company, exchanging waves and promising to get together soon. Nancy purposely avoided looking at Fletcher as she linked her arm through Brad's. From beneath her lashes she watched Fletcher cross the street, moving with his familiar lazy grace in spite of the cast, then ease himself into a silver sports car. As she and Brad walked to Brad's car, the sports car roared into action and disappeared around the corner.

Brad chuckled. "Fletch is quite a guy. You have to give him credit for not acting all high and mighty just because he's a McGill and loaded with bucks. That Shane won't give anyone the time of day, wouldn't even go to high school here. They shipped him off to a fancy boarding school in Atlanta. But Fletch? He fit right in, was one of the guys. And, Lord, could he get himself in trouble. He sure could throw a football, though. Finest quarterback Oakville ever had. He had scholarship offers, but his father said no dice. Fletch was a McGill. He didn't play football, he played executive at the mill."

"Fletcher hated working at the mill," Nancy said.

"Yeah, I know," Brad said, as they reached the car. He opened the door for her. "I wasn't surprised when he left here. I didn't think he'd last as long as he did." He assisted Nancy into the car, then walked around to slide behind the wheel. "I wonder," he went on, "why he came back. Even more, I wonder just what it is that he's been doing for six years."

"He said he was traveling around," Nancy said as Brad pulled away from the curb.

"I don't buy that. Fletch is too intelligent, too curious and energetic, to do the jet-set playboy routine for that long. Besides, that lifestyle costs plenty, and he—Never mind."

"He what?"

"I'm his banker, Nancy. It's confidential."

"Well, you've hinted that perhaps he didn't spend enough to indicate he was living the good life."

"Not a penny. Not one penny. That's off the record, okay? I'd be fired tomorrow for divulging a client's business, but from the day Fletch left Oakville, he didn't touch the money that was available to him. I don't know where he was or what he did, but he did it on his own. I'd say that Fletcher McGill has grown up."

"Yes, I . . . I see changes in him," Nancy said quietly.

"I didn't realize that you knew him that well. You're younger than we are."

"He helped out with Kip's Little League."

"Oh, yeah, that's right. Fletch spent a lot of time with those kids. I remember that now. Well, as I said, Fletch is quite a guy. It's good to have him home."

"He won't stay, Brad," she said, looking out the side window. "There's nothing here for him."

Brad shrugged. "Oh, you never know. People change. Fletch may be ready to settle down now. I'm not saying he'd ever work for his father. Those two are oil and water, but Fletch could have new career ideas for himself."

"In Oakville?" Nancy asked, turning to look at him.

"Nancy," Brad said, with a laugh, "with Fletcher McGill, *anything* is possible."

That, Nancy thought dryly, was the understatement of the year.

Fletcher decided that he felt like a total idiot. There he stood, hiding in the shadows next to Nance's house. It would be just his luck to have a neighbor catch sight of him and call the cops. Then Fletcher McGill would be in trouble again. Wonderful.

This was closest he'd ever gotten to Nance's house. He used to drive by it late at night, imagining her asleep in her bed, thinking of her, aching for her, but he'd never knocked on the front door and been invited inside. He'd hated it, the bitter distinction between the upper- and lower-income groups in that town.

The guys hadn't cared, he remembered. He was part of the team, more often than not the leader, and he was accepted as one of them. He'd been in their homes, eaten hamburgers grilled on barbecues in postage-stamp backyards. But two stubborn parents wouldn't give an inch: Nance's father, and Fletcher's. Fletcher refused to associate with the children of the executives at the mill, so he'd never brought his friends to the estate. And Nancy's father had always believed his children should stay with their own kind.

It had made him angry, Fletcher mused. All of it. And Nance would become sad. So very sad . . .

"Oh, Fletcher, I want you to have Sunday dinner with us. I want to look across the table and see you there, laughing and talking with my father and Kip. This is all so wrong. Why can't people be judged for who they are, instead of what they have?"

"Oakville is out of step, Nance, behind the times. If there were another big company here along with the mill, maybe it would be different. I don't know. I wish you wouldn't get so upset about it, sweetheart. Your father isn't going to change, and neither is mine. Each of them is a snob in his own way."

"I've tried to talk to Daddy about it. I've never mentioned your name, of course, just spoken in generalities. Oh, Fletcher, he gets so angry, tells me to stay away from the kids in the fancy houses and not to get highfalutin ideas about who I am and where I belong. If he could just talk to you, get to know you, he'd—"

"Shh, that's enough. It isn't going to happen. What's important is the two of us together. We're just Nance and Fletch, here at our pond. The birds, the squirrels, those croakin' old frogs, they don't

care how much money our families have. This is our world. Everyone else can go to hell. We don't need them."

"I just need you, Fletcher."

"That, my sweet Nancy, is what I've been trying to say. As long as we have each other, we've got it made."

"Don't ever leave me, Fletcher. Please. Don't ever leave me."

Fletcher leaned against the house and closed his eyes as Nancy's words, spoken so many years before, in a voice choked with tears, beat against his brain.

"Don't ever leave me, Fletcher."

Dammit, he thought, he *had* left her. Angry and hurt, cocky and arrogant, he'd stormed out of her life in a fit of temper that had matched his less-than-terrific level of maturity at the time. Now he could understand how frightened Nance had been at the prospect of running off with him in the middle of the night. He hadn't comprehended anything then except the fact that she refused to come with him. And she'd had six years to think about it. Six years to remember how cold and cruel he'd been. Six years, knowing he'd left her and hadn't come back.

Well, now he *was* back, he thought fiercely. Nance was his. He loved her as much as, if not more than, he had before. Hell, he loved her enough to be hiding in the shadows by her house like a Peeping Tom or a common thief. But he had to know what he was up against as far as Brad Sanders went. Brad was a good man and had a respectable job. He had a lot to offer Nance, and Fletcher had to know how serious their relationship was. Nancy was adamant about leaving Oakville, but if Brad was in love with her, could convince her to marry him and stay, then—No way. There was no way in hell that Nancy Forest was marrying Brad Sanders!

Fletcher was pulled from this thoughts by the sound of a car in the driveway. He inched closer to the edge of the house and peered around.

Damn, he thought, they were talking by the car, and he couldn't hear a thing they were saying. They sure were taking their sweet time about ending the evening, for Pete's sake. Come on, Sanders, go home, he urged silently.

As Nancy and Brad started toward the house, Fletcher ducked back around the corner.

"Of course I'll miss you when I move to Atlanta, Brad," Fletcher heard Nancy say. "You're my dear friend. Here's my key."

Dear friend, Fletcher thought, nodding in approval. She was Fletcher McGill's woman. He hoped.

"I'll miss you, too, Nancy," Brad said.

Fletcher stiffened as several silent seconds passed. The bum was kissing her! he raged.

He peered around the corner of the house. Dammit to hell! Brad had her plastered against him and was kissing her as if there were no tomorrow. He was going to take that Brad Sanders apart limb by limb. Enough, already. Did Brad want Nancy to pass out from lack of oxygen? He'd give them two more seconds; then he'd—

"Good night, Brad," Nancy said.

It's about time, Fletcher thought, ducking back around the corner. That was a helluva kiss she'd let him get away with, considering he was only supposed to be her dear friend.

"I'll call you soon," Brad said.

"Thanks again. 'Bye," Nancy said.

"Good night."

Haul it, Sanders, Fletcher mentally directed.

A car door slammed, an engine was started. As Fletcher peered around the corner again, he saw the taillights of Brad's car disappear down the street. Fletcher sent Brad another mental message not to notice Fletcher's sports car, parked two blocks away.

He emerged from the shadows, stepped up on the porch, and knocked lightly on the door, suddenly wondering what he was going to say if Kip answered.

Nancy had not bothered to turn on a light when she'd entered the house and locked the door behind her. The moonlight inching through the drapes that had never quite closed properly illuminated a path to her bedroom. She had just entered her room and tossed her purse onto the dresser, when a soft knock sounded at the front door.

Brad? she wondered, turning around. Had he forgotten something? Oh, dear, he wasn't going to propose again, was he? She hadn't wanted to hurt him, but his continuous urgings to marry him had forced her to tell him that she just didn't love him.

The knock came again. It wouldn't wake Kip. He slept like the dead. Whoever was at the door apparently wasn't going to go away.

Nancy left the bedroom and retraced her steps to the door, leaning close to it. "Who is it?" she asked.

"Fletcher."

Fletcher. Fletcher? On her porch? What on earth for?

"Nance, open the door."

"Why?"

"Because I'm knocking on it. When someone knocks on your door, you open it to see what he wants. That's the polite thing to do."

"Forget polite. What do you want?"

"To talk to you."

"Why?"

"Dammit, open the door!"

"Fletcher McGill, keep your voice down. If you wake my neighbors, I'm going to wring your neck."

"I'm going to count to five, Nance. If this door isn't open, I'm going to start singing 'Roll Me Over in the Clover' at the top of my lungs."

"You wouldn't dare."

"One . . . two . . . I would definitely dare, Nancy . . . three . . . four . . ."

She flung the door open, then planted her hands on her hips as she glared up at him.

"Hi," he said, flashing her a dazzling smile. "Yes, thank you, I'd love to come in."

"You are not coming—Oh!" She gasped as two large hands gripped her waist and lifted her off her feet. In the next instant Fletcher had moved her back into the room, set her down, and kicked the door shut with his uninjured foot. "Good Lord, you're rude," she said. "Pushy and rude. Leave this house."

"No."

'Darn it, Fletcher, what do you want? This is insane."

"You're beautiful in the moonlight," he said, his voice low. "It's pouring over you like a silver waterfall."

"Now, look, Fletcher, I—"

"Do you realize," he interrupted, looking directly

into her eyes, "that I'm here, in your living room, for the first time? We talked about this, remember? We hated the prejudices in Oakville, the invisible line drawn down the street and covered with dollar signs. We're all grown-up now, Nance. We're free to live, free to love. And I do love you, Nancy."

"No," she said, shaking her head. She wrapped her arms around her waist in a protective gesture and took a step backward. "I don't want to hear that."

"Why not? It's true."

"Oh? That's why it took you six years to come home? Because you love me so very much?"

"I told you, Nance. I was sure you were gone. You did leave after I did. It's only because Kip needed you that you came back. Hell, Nancy, I know I made mistakes, hurt you, hurt my mother, by disappearing for so long. A lot of things happened while I was away. I changed, grew up, figured out who I was and what I was meant to do with my life."

"What happened? What things?"

"That's not important right now. What *is* important is that you believe me when I say that I love you."

"What difference does it make?" she asked, her voice rising. "I'm leaving here, Fletcher. I'm going to have *my* turn at finding out who I am and what I was meant to do with my life. I won't be swayed by emotions, yours or mine. I'm not going to try to figure out if you really do still love me, because I don't want to know."

"And *your* emotions, Nancy?" he asked. He stepped closer and trailed his thumb over her cheek. Nancy shivered from the feathery foray. "Are you going to get in touch with yourself and discover how you feel about me?"

"No," she whispered, shaking her head.

"That won't work, you know," he said, moving even closer to her. "Love doesn't just go quietly away if you ignore it. It's there in your heart, your mind, your soul. It causes desire to churn inside you; hot desire, a burning need to be one with that other person. Are you burning, Nance? Are you?"

"Stop it," she said as her knees began to tremble.

"So beautiful in the moonlight," he murmured, lowering his head toward hers.

Move, Nancy! she order herself frantically. Hurry. He was going to—

He kissed her.

Too late, she thought as her eyes drifted closed.

Fletcher claimed her mouth in unhurried pleasure, parting her lips, finding her tongue, savoring her taste and feel and sweet, feminine aroma. As she wrapped her arms around his neck, he knew she was also claiming his heart and soul with all that she was. Nance. His Nancy. He gathered her to him, crushing her breasts to his chest, and the kiss intensified.

Whispers of heat licked through Nancy as she molded herself to the hard contours of Fletcher's body. She was touching, tasting, feeling, what had only been memories for so very long. The kiss by the pond had been but a mere sample of the ecstasy they could share. She could define every rugged inch of him as she leaned further into his heat. She remembered it all, wanted it all, had to have it all. Fletcher's sensual promise caused a soft purr to escape from her throat.

The passionate sound slammed against Fletcher's mind, causing his blood to pound in his veins and his manhood to surge. He slid his hands beneath Nancy's lightweight sweater, relishing the softness of her skin. Then up, to cup the sides of her small breasts, his thumbs inching forward to stroke the nipples, which grew taut against the wispy fabric of her bra. He tore his lips from hers, then trailed nibbling kisses down her throat as he strove for control.

"Oh, Fletcher," Nancy said breathlessly, going nearly limp in his arms. "I feel so . . . so . . ."

"We're good together, Nancy," he said, his voice rough with passion, "and I do love you, I swear I do." He lifted his head to meet her gaze, his thumbs never stopping their tantalizing journey over her breasts. "Give me a chance. Give us a chance to reclaim what's ours, what we had that summer. Those feelings aren't gone. They're waiting for us. They're ours to have."

Nancy sighed, and to Fletcher it was a sad, sad sound, one of hurt and confusion, mingled with the desire he'd created within her. He clenched his teeth and drew his hands from beneath her sweater as he took a step backward. Nancy looked at him; she was clearly puzzled.

"Not until you're sure," he said, attempting a smile that failed. "When we make love again it's going to be perfect for both of us. There's no room in our world for regrets over something that's so incredibly beautiful between us. That's how much I love you, Nancy. I won't satisfy my own needs, and I won't run roughshod over your sense of reason. It's too important to me, to us. Nothing is going to happen until you're very sure it's what you want."

"Fletcher, I—"

"Shh." He brushed his lips over hers. "Good night. Dream about me. Not the ant. Me. I love you."

He stepped out of the circle of silvery moonlight into the darkness; then Nancy heard the door close quietly behind him.

She pressed trembling fingers to her kiss-swollen lips and drew a steadying breath. Her body hummed with desire, ached for fulfillment. Her breasts throbbed from Fletcher's touch. And he had wanted her, she knew, for she'd felt the evidence of his arousal pressing against her, promising the ecstasy she yearned for.

Fletcher, the boy, she realized, would have made love to her. Fletcher, the man, had gathered his control and stepped back, waiting for her to be certain she was ready to be one with him again.

She walked slowly into her bedroom, knowing that sleep would be elusive. This was a side of Fletcher she'd never seen, a level of maturity that hadn't been there before. Now what? she wondered, sinking onto her bed. Would Fletcher sit on the McGill estate, waiting for her to call and say, "Dah-ling, I've thought it over, and I've decided we really ought to do it in the grass at Fletcher's Pond"? Oh, for heaven's sake, how disgusting.

"Good grief," she said, yanking her sweater over her head. Did he truly love her? Did his walking away when he obviously could have made love to her mean more than if they'd actually made love? Oh, she didn't know. It was all too confusing.

She prepared for bed, then lay staring up into the darkness, replaying in her mind all that had happened since she'd opened the door to Fletcher. She had told him she didn't care whether or not he still loved her. But deep within her, she asked herself, didn't she want to know? No. Yes. It shouldn't matter! She was leaving Oakville. She was going to follow her own dreams, live her own life. She was resigned—not happy about it—but resigned to taking the memories, the love for Fletcher, with her in her heart and soul. Still, it shouldn't matter how he felt about her.

"Enough," she said, squeezing her eyes closed. She couldn't think about this any more tonight. Brad said that he loved her, Fletcher said that he loved her, and she just wanted to be left alone. It was time to start thinking about the exciting job waiting for her at Cory Computer. She needed to sort through her things and pack what she wished to take with her from the house, make a thorough inventory of her wardrobe to see if she was ready for her new career. There was no room in her life for confusion, doubt, and unanswered questions caused by Fletcher McGill. She was going to be very busy getting ready to leave Oakville, Georgia.

"That's right," she said decisively, and wiggled into a more comfortable position.

In her dream, Fletcher was wearing a cowboy outfit, with boots, a Stetson, and six-shooters. He came galloping up to Fletcher's Pond, sitting high in the saddle, on a gigantic ant.

Four

When Fletcher arrived at the terrace door the next morning, his step faltered slightly. His father was sitting at the table with Shane and his mother.

There they were, Fletcher thought dryly, the perfect southern family, complete with a dutiful son who had made no waves, who still lived under the master's thumb, where he would bring his bride someday and tell her she was never to be mistress of her own home.

And here *he* was, Fletcher thought, the black sheep, the thorn in their side. Fletch the rebel, the misfit, the troublemaker, home to stir up the quiet waters. Easy, Fletch. He had to stay cool for his mother's sake. The chip on his shoulder mustn't be allowed to take shape.

"Good morning," Fletcher said as he approached the table. His father turned, then got slowly to his feet. "Hello, Dad. I didn't know you were back."

Fletcher stopped in front of his father and extended his hand. He looked old, Fletcher thought suddenly. Old and tired. No one else he'd seen since he'd been back seemed to have changed very much, except Dennis McGill.

"I just arrived an hour ago," Dennis said. He hesitated a moment, then shook hands with Fletcher.

"Sit down, Fletcher," Elsie said. "Have some breakfast."

"I'm going to the mill," Shane said, rising.

"Don't let me run you off," Fletcher said pleasantly.

"Some of us around here work for a living." There was a sharp edge to Shane's voice.

"That's nice," Fletcher said, smiling at his brother, then sitting in the chair Shane had vacated. "Have a good one."

"I'll be in later, Shane," Dennis said, sitting down again.

"Fine," Shane said, then strode from the terrace with heavy steps.

"Why don't you leave me and Fletcher for a bit, Elsie?" Dennis said. "You might see to the unpacking of my luggage."

"Oh," Elsie said, fiddling with the string of pearls at her throat. "Well, yes, of course, I'll do that right now." She glanced quickly at Dennis, then at Fletcher. Fletcher smiled and winked at her before she hurried into the house.

Fletcher stirred sugar into his coffee, then propped his elbows on the table and cradled the cup in his hands. He took a sip as he looked directly at his father. Dennis was staring at him, no readable expression on his face. Silent seconds ticked by.

"How's the ankle doing?" Dennis finally asked.

"My ankle?" Fletcher said, startled by the question. "Oh, it's fine. The worst was over before I came back."

"Your mother said you never really explained how you broke it."

"I didn't want to upset her. The story is a bit dramatic."

Dennis frowned. "Don't you think, Fletcher, that you upset her when you disappeared in the middle of the night and didn't return for six years?"

"Yes," he said without hesitation. "It wasn't fair to her. She deserved better."

"Did I?"

Fletcher sighed and set his cup down. "If I'd come to you, told you I was leaving, we would have argued. We managed to argue over just about everything in those days."

"You've got a point there," Dennis said, and chuckled softly. Fletcher's eyes widened. "We did rattle a few windows in our time. That's the McGill temper meeting the McGill temper. You were a handful to raise, Fletcher."

"I wasn't bad," Fletcher said, smiling slightly. "I was busy, that's all. Kept all of you on your toes."

"That's putting it mildly," Dennis said, pouring himself more coffee. "If I asked you where you've been and what you've been doing for the past six years, would you tell me?"

"No, sir, not yet. When the time is right I will, but not yet."

"Then I won't ask."

Fletcher slouched back in his chair. "Why not? Damn, you're making me nervous. I expected you to hand me my head, and you're sitting here as if we're chatting about the weather. Look, I had to leave, okay? I shouldn't have hurt Mom the way I did, but I couldn't stay here any more."

"I understand that."

"You do? That's crazy." His voice started to rise. "I owe you an explanation. I owe you . . . something. Hell, I don't know."

"No, Fletcher, you don't owe me a damn thing. I'm the one with debts to pay."

"What are you talking about?"

"I tried to mold you like a lump of clay, turn you into another obedient son like Shane. I tried to break your spirit, and I had no right to do that. Damn, I've missed you, boy. Shane practically salutes me, never questions my directives, never gives me any argument or input. It's just, 'Yes, sir,' 'Right away, sir.' I've often wanted to yell at him, to say, 'Fight back, you milquetoast. Give me an opinion, at least.' He's as exciting as soggy cereal."

Fletcher burst into laughter. "I can't believe this."

"I'm a McGill. You're a McGill." Dennis shook his head. "I'm not sure what Shane is. He takes after your mother's side of the family, I guess. She never crosses me, either. Don't misunderstand—I love your mother and your brother. But it took your leaving to make me see how much I needed the challenge of taking you on. It's been damn quiet here. I feel old, finished, as though there's nothing new around the corner. I don't suppose you'd like to come back to the mill and raise a little hell, would you?"

"No," Fletcher said, smiling, "but thanks for the offer. I don't belong at the mill, Dad."

"I know, but it's a shame. Are you staying in Oakville, Fletcher?"

"I don't know, Dad It depends on—It depends."

"On a woman?"

Fletcher looked at his father for a long moment before he answered. "Yes."

"Does she love you?"

"I'm not sure. I hurt her very badly when I left."

"But women, bless them, have gentle and forgiving hearts."

"I hope so."

"Do you know what you want to do with your life?"

"Yes. I've been doing it for many years now. Dad, I want to tell her first, okay? Can you understand that?"

"Of course."

"You know, I never thought this moment would come between you and me. It's as though you've finally accepted me for who I am."

"I have, son," Dennis said, his voice oddly husky. "I love you, boy."

"I don't know what to say to you, Dad. I never really knew you, I realize that now. You're accepting me, not even knowing where I've been or what I've been doing. I can't begin to tell you what that means to me."

"We should have had this talk years ago. It took your leaving to make me see what I had, really had, in you. All I can say is, welcome home, son. I've missed you."

When Elsie McGill came to the terrace door, tears quickly filled her eyes. Her husband and son were holding each other in a bone-crushing hug.

• • •

That evening after dinner, Nancy stood in the living room, holding a large, empty carton.

"What's up?" Kip asked, wandering into the room, eating an apple.

"I have to start sorting and packing. You know, deciding what I want to take with me."

"Don't you think you should find a place to live first? Then you'd know what could fit where."

"Well, I have to have some knickknacks, and stuff. I can hardly wait to move to Atlanta. I can go to concerts, plays, visit museums, and . . . and have a wonderful time."

"A wonderful time," Kip repeated, frowning. "You look like you just found out you're going to Atlanta to attend a funeral. What's wrong, Nancy?"

She dropped the box onto the floor, sighed, then flopped onto the sofa. "I'm just tired. I didn't sleep very well last night."

"Then don't start packing now."

"Yes, I *am* going to start," she said, jumping to her feet. "I need to make it clear that I'm really leaving Oakville."

"Clear to who?" Kip asked, obviously confused. "Everybody knows that you're going to Atlanta to work for Cory Computer. Clear to who?"

"Me," she said, splaying her hand on her chest.

"You're not making any sense."

"No," she said softly, "I suppose I'm not. Never mind, Kip. I'm in a strange mood, and I'm tired. You're right, this isn't the time to start packing."

"Look, I was going over to Bernie's to study, but I can stay here if you'd rather not be alone. I've never seen you like this, Nancy."

"I'm fine," she said, forcing a smile. "You go ahead with your plans. I'll take a long bubble bath, then go to bed early. All I need is a good night's sleep. Dad used to say that, remember? Put your problems on the shelf until you've had a good night's sleep."

"Are you sure you don't want me to stay here with you?"

"Positive. Go. Take the rest of those brownies with you to snack on."

"Well, okay. I won't be late."

After Kip had collected his books and the brownies and left the house, Nancy stood in the silent living room staring at the empty carton.

Poor Kip, she thought. He had a nut case for a sister. There she'd stood with her pathetic little box, claiming all would be well if she stuffed some junk into it. Good heavens, what was wrong with her? She'd been in a state of near-panic all day as visions of Fletcher taunted her, along with the remembrance of his kiss, his touch, the feel of his body pressed to hers. She'd heard in echoing whispers in her mind, over and over, his declarations of love for her, saw the desire and tenderness in his expression. He had beckoned to her in her mind's eye all through the long hours, urging her to come to him, be with him for as long as he chose, this time, to be with *her.*

She wasn't excited about Atlanta, or packing her first box, or looking through the Atlanta newspaper she'd bought to see what kind of apartments were available. She wasn't excited at all. She was a confused, muddled mess. For every mental step she took toward Atlanta, the thought of Fletcher pulled her back two steps. Back and back, until she was caught, trapped, held in place until he left again, until Fletcher decided she could be free to live her own life.

"No," she said, shaking her head, "he isn't going to do this to me." Her first instinct was to be angry at Fletcher. Angry because he'd come back when she was so very close to leaving. Angry because the changes she saw and sensed in him made him even more appealing. Angry because . . . because he was Fletcher.

But, she reluctantly admitted, the blame for her emotional upheaval lay squarely on her own shoulders. Her own weakness and susceptibility to the memories of Fletcher and his vibrant masculinity were causing her distress. Those, and the fact that she still loved him. She was so mad at herself, she could have screamed.

"I'm too tired to scream," she said, throwing up her hands.

She opened the front door to see a gorgeous sunset streaking across the sky in rippling waves of color. She was drawn to the beautiful spectacle, and went outside, sitting down on the top porch step.

Ten minutes later, Fletcher's sports car pulled into her driveway.

Why not? Nancy thought, wondering if she was becoming hysterical. He'd been prancing around in her head all day, so why not show up in person? It was perfectly reasonable. And he was perfectly beautiful. Tight jeans, knit shirt the exact brown shade of his eyes . . . beautiful.

"Hello," Fletcher said, stopping in front of her. "May I join you?"

"If you like," she said. He wasn't smiling, but then, neither was she.

He lowered himself next to her on the step, stretched out his injured leg, and bent the other one at the knee.

"Is Kip here?" he asked. "I'd like to say hello to him."

"No, he's studying at a friend's," she said, still looking at the sky. He smelled good, she thought, like soap and a light lime after-shave. "You saw Kip at your house. He's part of the landscaping crew."

"I saw him? You're kidding. He must have really changed."

"He's very tall. It's understandable that you didn't recognize him."

"Why didn't he tell me who he was?"

"You startled him, Fletcher. He saw a coldness in your eyes that hadn't been there before. I've seen it myself."

Fletcher shrugged.

"Okay, I won't push. Where you've been, what you've done or seen, is your business."

Only for now, Fletcher thought. He desperately needed to have her accept him just for himself, as the man who loved her. He didn't want to muddy the waters with what he'd done, where he'd been, for the past six years. He wanted their relationship to be based on love, pure and simple. Love and trust. Man to woman. Woman to man. Nance and Fletch, as in the days at Fletcher's Pond.

"I saw my father today," he said quietly. "He just got back from a business trip, so it was our first meeting in six years."

"It's a wonder I didn't hear the two of you hollering way down in town."

"It wasn't like that, Nance. We talked, really talked, for the first time in our lives. I always loved him, but I sure didn't like him. Now I like him, understand him, and respect him."

Nancy turned to look at him. "I'm very happy for you, Fletcher. I mean that. I know how distressing it was for you always to be at crossed swords with your father. Did you . . . tell him where you'd been and what you'd done?"

"No. I wasn't ready to," he said, looking directly into her eyes. "He accepted that. And he accepted me."

"Why are you being so secretive about these past several years, Fletcher?"

"I'm not."

"Then tell me."

"No."

"Why not?"

"Because it isn't time, Nance. Things need to take place in the proper order."

"You're talking in riddles."

"Yeah, I guess it sounds that way. Let's drop it for now. How was your day?"

Don't ask, she thought glumly. "Fine. I'm very eager to move to Atlanta. I even have a box in the living room so I can start packing. You do know that I have a job at Cory Computer, don't you? Oh, goodness, there are just so many exciting, fun, interesting things waiting for me in Atlanta."

"Like men?"

"Oodles of men," she said, staring up at the sky again.

"What are you trying to do? Set a record?" he asked much too loudly. "You've already had me and Brad kissing the socks off you, both in the same night."

She stared at him. "You were watching Brad and me?"

Uh-oh, Fletcher thought.

"How dare you, Fletcher McGill. Where were you?"

"Sort of . . . in the vicinity," he said lamely.

"That's despicable."

"Oh, yeah? What would you call that kiss you let 'dear friend' Brad lay on you? Now we're getting to the nitty-gritty of despicable." Hell. When was he going to learn to keep his mouth shut?

"Get off my porch, Fletcher."

"No," he said sullenly.

"Yes."

"No. I've waited too many years to sit on this porch, to be welcome in your home. You're not tossing me out of here just because you're in a snit. Don't you remember how much you wanted me to have Sunday dinner with you? Well, here I am. Invite me to Sunday dinner."

"I certainly will not."

"What are you afraid of, Nance?" he asked, his voice suddenly low and intense. "Me? I've never given you any reason to fear me. I think you're afraid of yourself, of what you might discover about your feelings for me. Or, heaven forbid, you may have to face the truth and acknowledge that I love you. Why does all of that frighten you, Nancy. Why?"

"It doesn't." Oh, dear Lord, yes, it did. "It just doesn't matter, that's all." It couldn't matter. She wouldn't allow it to, because she was leaving. "I'm leaving, remember?"

"Oh, yeah, that's right," he said dryly. "You're off to Atlanta and the oodles of men."

"Yep. Oodles."

"How many men have there been in your bed in the past six years, Nancy? Is Brad one of them?"

"Oh, that caps it," she said, narrowing her eyes and getting to her feet. "I'm going inside. You can sit on this step until doomsday, for all I care."

Fletcher sighed. "Nance, wait. I'm sorry. I didn't mean to say that. The fact that you've slept with Brad Sanders is none of my business."

"I have not slept with Brad Sanders," she said. She plopped back down onto the step so she could glare directly into his face. "Or anyone else, for that matter. You have a dirty, tacky mind."

"There's been no one?" he asked, a smile creeping slowly onto his face. "No one but me?" The smile grew bigger.

"Don't you hear well? I just said . . . Oh, now, wait a minute here. You did that on purpose. You tricked me into telling you exactly what you wanted to know."

"Just gathering data, my sweet," he said, tapping his temple with his finger. "The question remains, though—*why* hasn't there been anyone since me? Would you care to answer that? Speak right into the microphone, my dear, so all our viewers at home can hear you."

"McGill, take a hike."

Fletcher hooted with laughter, then quieted as a battered pickup truck pulled next to the curb.

"It's Kip," Nancy said.

"That's Kip? You weren't kidding when you said

he'd grown. Hey, Kip," he called, "how are you? Lord, doesn't Nancy feed you? You're no bigger than when I saw you last. You're a real runt."

A wide smile split Kip's face, and he sprinted forward, shaking Fletcher's hand vigorously when he reached the steps.

"Damn, it's good to see you, Fletcher," Kip said.

"Don't swear," Nancy said.

"I saw you at your house, but I thought . . . Forget that. You're the Fletcher I know. I was crazy to think you could change that much. Man, what a shock to see you on our front steps. You've never been here before."

"Yeah, well, that's an old, sad story," Fletcher said. "I just dropped by to see how you were, and to tell Nancy that I love her, and to—"

"What?" Nancy and Kip said in unison.

Fletcher got to his feet. "The way I see it, Kip, you're the man of the family now. So, with all due respect to your title and role, I'm going on record as having informed you that I am in love with your sister, one Miss Nancy Forest. I have been in love with said sister for over six years."

"Oh, good Lord," Nancy said, clamping her hand over her eyes.

"No joke?" Kip asked, beaming from ear to ear.

"No joke."

"Someone tell me this isn't happening," Nancy said, peering through her fingers. "I can't handle this."

"Then why did you take off for so long?" Kip asked Fletcher, suddenly frowning.

"Out of the mouths of babes," Nancy muttered.

"That's another sad story," Fletcher answered. "Anyway, now you know the scoop, which you have the right to know, because— "

"He's the man of the family." Nancy dropped her hand and rolled her eyes heavenward.

"Right," Fletcher said. "Thing is, Kip, I have this problem, because Nance—I call her Nance—Nance doesn't believe that I still love her, since I have a lousy track record. However, I'm working on that. I guess that about brings you up-to-date."

"Oh," Kip said, appearing rather dazed.

"Hell," Nancy said.

"Don't swear, Nance. You're setting a bad example for the young man who is head of the family here. Well, I'd better shove off." He swept Nancy into his arms, bent her over backward, and planted a searing kiss on her mouth. She staggered slightly when he released her. "See y'all," he said, and headed for his car.

As the sports car roared off down the street, Nancy marched up the steps. "Don't say one word to me, Kip. Not one, single word."

"Hey, that's not fair," he protested, following close on her heels. "I'm the man of the family, you know. I need a few details here."

Nancy shot him a dark look over her shoulder before going into the house. She sat down on the sofa, got up again, and began to pace the floor.

"I can't believe the audacity of that Fletcher McGill," she said, nearly sputtering. "How dare he say such a thing to my very own brother in my very own front yard? How dare he kiss me in front of my very own brother in my very own front yard? I bet the neighbors were watching. I just bet they were. By tomorrow, everyone will know what took place in my—"

"Very own front yard," Kip finished for her, then dissolved in a fit of laughter.

"Kip Forest, you be quiet," Nancy yelled. "This isn't funny."

"Sorry."

"You are not. You're grinning."

"Fletcher McGill in love with my sister," Kip said. "That just blows my mind. And he has loved you since before he went away? Unreal. Do you love him, Nancy? I mean, if you do, and he's back, and he still loves you, why are you planning to move to Atlanta by yourself? Why aren't you making plans to be with Fletcher?"

Nancy stopped pacing and planted her hands on her hips. "In the first place, young man, I never said that I still . . . that I have any feelings for Mr. McGill. In the second place, I'm going to Atlanta because I want to, because it's my turn to live my own life. And in the third place, it's none of your business."

"Wrong. It *is* my business. As Fletcher pointed out, *I* am the man of this family. I can see now that I've neglected my duties. I'm nearly eighteen years old. I have a responsibility here. Yes, sir, I've got to get my act together."

"Would you stop? Being nearly eighteen years old doesn't make you the man of this family or . . ." Nancy's voice trailed off. Yes, it did. Kip *was* the man of the family at nearly eighteen. When she had been eighteen she'd been a woman, Fletcher's woman, in love, making love at Fletcher's Pond. That wasn't her baby brother standing there; it was a young man on the brink of adulthood who was about to go out into the world alone. She couldn't scold him and send him to his room, not anymore. He was all grown up, her Kip. "Yes, you're right," she said quietly. "You *are* the man of this house, Kipper."

"I am? Oh, I mean, yes, of course, I am." He paused. "Therefore!" he boomed. Nancy jumped. "I would like to know what you plan to do about Fletcher McGill."

"I'm going to Atlanta. Alone."

"Do you love him?"

"It isn't important."

"You love him," Kip said, nodding.

"I never said that!"

"You didn't have to. I can tell. Six years ago. Man, you weren't much older than I am. Holy smokes, you were sneaking around to see Fletcher, right? Dad would have pitched a fit if he'd known."

"I'd prefer not to discuss it," she said, staring at a spot on the wall.

"What I don't get is, if he loved you then, and you loved *him* then, why did he leave you for six years?"

"Because I wouldn't go . . . I mean . . . Forget it."

"You wouldn't go with him? He asked you to, but you wouldn't go? Why the hell not?"

"Don't swear," she said, glaring at him.

"Why didn't you go?"

"I was scared to death, Kip. For Pete's sake, I was only eighteen. Fletcher wanted us to run off in the middle of the night, just disappear. I couldn't do it, so he got angry, he was hurt, and he went himself."

"Wow," Kip said, sinking onto the sofa. "That is really something. Nobody in this town knew about you two. And now he's back, and he still loves you. Wow. But this time *you're* running out on *him*."

"I am not."

"What would you call it?"

"My plans were made long before I knew he was coming back."

"So change them."

"No. Fletcher doesn't settle anywhere, Kip. He said that he's been traveling around for six years. Granted, I believe there's more to it than that, but it doesn't erase the fact that he's restless, always on the move. Love or no love, that's not the kind of life I want."

"So tell him that."

"No."

"Have you told him that you still love him?"

"No."

"Geez."

"There's no point to it, Kip. It won't change anything. Fletcher and I are just too different. I hate to break this to you, but love does not conquer all. He'll be leaving Oakville soon, I'm sure of it, and I'm going to Atlanta. That will be that. I doubt if I'll ever see Fletcher again after that."

"That's lousy."

"That," she said, with a sigh, "is life. I'm going to go take a bubble bath, then go to bed. Lock up the house, okay?"

"Yeah, sure, I'll take care of it."

"Good night, Kip," she said, starting toward her room.

"Nancy?"

"Yes?" She turned to look at him.

"You know that I think our dad was top-notch, really first-rate."

"Yes. Yes, he was."

"Well, in my opinion, Fletcher McGill ranks right up there at the head of the list, too, equal billing with our father. You lost one of the good guys because of death. I sure hope you know what you're doing about the other one."

"You grew up when I wasn't looking, Kipper. Good night."

Darkness fell, crickets serenaded in the night, frogs croaked in accompaniment, but Fletcher made no move to leave Fletcher's Pond. He gathered the memories of all that had transpired in that secret, special place into his heart, his mind, his soul. He savored each image, feeling the warmth it created flow through him like brandy.

Slowly, reluctantly, he pulled himself back to the present, to the scene that had taken place in Nancy's front yard.

Well, he thought dryly, he was either a genius or an idiot, and only time would give him the answer. Time. That was one of his enemies. The days were passing, and Nance was moving forward with her plans to leave Oakville. She was not accepting or acknowledging his love for her or any feelings she had for him. Damn.

And so he'd boldly announced to Kip that Fletcher McGill was in love with Nancy Forest. In that house, at least, it was out in the open, and would be talked about, if he was any judge of young men. Kip would push for details. Nancy, he hoped, would admit to her brother that she did indeed still love Fletcher. Words spoken aloud were harder to run from.

It was a long shot at best, Fletcher knew, but he was getting desperate. There was no chance at all of a future with Nancy if she stayed hidden behind her protective walls. There'd be no way to show her who he'd become, what he could now offer her, if she closed her eyes and ears, her heart, to all that he was.

So, Fletcher mused, he'd started with Kip. If that didn't work, he'd press further, from one end of Oakville, Georgia, to the other!

"A genius or an idiot?" he asked the night.

But neither the crickets nor the frogs answered.

Five

The next day after work Nancy drove to the high school. The baseball team was playing a double-header against a visiting school, and the extra game would give her a chance to see Kip play. The bleachers were crowded, many people having taken advantage of thc fact that the sports event would still be going on after the normal workday.

"Kip's playing like a pro," someone yelled to Nancy as she worked her way across the bleachers. She waved, then settled herself in an empty seat.

"Third inning," she mumbled. "No score."

"We won the first one," said Mr. Hansen, who owned the drugstore. "It was a beauty. Kip hit a triple and a double. He's out there in center field. See him?"

"Yes." Nancy smiled. "I see him."

After that inning, the next two went by with little excitement; batters up, batters out. The cheerleaders pranced around shouting their chants, and a rather off-key pep band played at whim. As she always did when Kip was playing, Nancy became totally engrossed in the game, blocking out the noise of the crowd and the general commotion in the stands.

When a deep, husky voice whispered in her ear, she gasped in surprise. "Hi."

She turned her head and was nearly nose to nose with Fletcher, who was now sitting next to her. Who was smiling at her. Whose brown eyes were gazing into hers. Who looked fantastic and gave off a heady aroma of soap and after-shave and male perspiration.

Nancy swallowed. "What . . . are you doing here?"

"I came to watch our boy play. I've known Kip had something special going for him since he was a little kid."

"Oh," Nancy said weakly. They were sitting so close, and Fletcher's warm, peppermint-scented breath had feathered against her lips as he'd spoken to her, causing a funny flutter in the pit of her stomach.

"But then," Fletcher went on, "both of you Forests have something special going for you."

"Oh," Nancy said again, nearly mesmerized by Fletcher's softly spoken words and the proximity of his body.

Fletcher chuckled. "Watch the game." He paused. "And I'll watch you watch the game."

She snapped out of her semitrance. "Don't be absurd," she said, redirecting her attention to the field. "Oh, Kip's up to bat."

"Yep."

"Let's go, batter," Nancy yelled. "Show 'em where

you live, Forest. Hit that baby right out of here. Come on, batter, batter, batter."

"Good Lord," Fletcher said, laughing.

"You have to get into the spirit of things," Nancy explained, her eyes riveted on Kip.

"Strike one," the umpire hollered.

"You're blind, ump," Nancy said, jumping to her feet.

"Sit down, Nancy," someone said. "I hate it when I get a seat behind you."

"Sorry." Nancy plopped back down.

"Strike two!"

Nancy was up and on her feet again. "Are you nuts?"

"Nancy, sit down," three people said in unison. She sat.

"Easy, dear," Fletcher said, patting her on the knee. "Don't overexcite yourself." She shot him a stormy glare.

Crack!

"He hit it!" Nancy said, up again. "Kip hit it. Go. Run. Faster. Kipper, move!"

"Nope," Fletcher said.

"Out!" Nancy shrieked. "What do you mean, out? He reached first base before the ball did, you ding-dong." Kip trotted back to the dugout. "You were safe by a mile, Kip," she yelled at him. "I have witnesses."

Fletcher laughed, and tugged on her arm until she sat back down.

"They're going to toss you out of here," he said, grinning at her. "I'm not sure that Oakville is ready for so much enthusiasm."

"Everyone knows when Nancy's at a game," Mr.

Hansen said, chuckling. "They probably know it in the next county."

"Kip was safe," Nancy said.

"Kip was out," Fletcher said.

"Was not," she said. "How did you see it, Mr. Hansen?"

"Oh, now, leave me out of this," Mr. Hansen said. "I made the mistake of arguing a call with you once, Nancy. I'll leave you in Fletcher's hands. If anyone can control your excitement, he can."

Fletcher leaned closer to Nancy. "You heard the man," he whispered. "You're being put in my hands. You remember my hands, don't you, Nance? Do I know how to control your excitement? Oh, I surely do. I know just where to touch you, where to—"

"Stop it," she said, smacking him on the knee as she felt a warm flush on her cheeks.

"Think about it," he said, then looked at the field again. "By the way, you're blushing."

"I am not," she said, much too loudly.

"You're not what?" someone behind her asked.

"Forget it," Nancy muttered. Fletcher chuckled.

The game proceeded, with Nancy jumping to her feet, people telling her to sit down, and Fletcher breaking into laughter when she loudly disputed calls. There was no score at the top of the ninth inning, when Kip came up to bat.

"His stance is off," Fletcher said. "Pull in your left foot, Kip," he muttered under his breath.

"Left foot?" Nancy repeated, leaning forward.

"Come on, kid." Fletcher frowned. "Pull it in."

"Strike one!"

"Damn," Fletcher said. "Where's the coach? Has he lost his voice? Hell."

"Strike two!"

Fletcher stood up. "Left foot, Kip," he bellowed.

Kip stepped out of the batter's box, picked up a handful of dirt, and looked up into the stands. Fletcher made several motions with his hands. Kip nodded, tugged his cap firmly into place, and stepped back into the batter's box. Fletcher sat down, and Nancy grabbed his hand in both of hers.

"There," Fletcher said. "Now he's got it. Give 'em hell, Kip."

Crack! The ball went sailing. The crowd roared its approval, and *everyone* was on his feet.

Home run!

"Hooray!" Nancy said, flinging her arms around Fletcher's neck. "He did it. You did it. You both did it."

Fletcher gave her a hard, fast kiss. Nancy was so flustered that she dropped her arms from his neck and turned to stare at the field. As Kip rounded the bases, the crowd applauded and cheered its congratulations. Kip saluted Fletcher as he headed for the dugout, and Fletcher gave him a thumbs-up sign.

Nancy honestly didn't remember the remainder of the game. Her mind was whirling with conflicting emotions. Had a lot of people seen Fletcher kiss her? Would they place any importance on it, or merely chalk it up to the excitement of the moment? Did it matter what they thought? She was an adult, not a child. It was no one's business if Fletcher kissed her at a baseball game.

It was such fun, she thought, to be at the game with Fletcher, cheering Kip on together. "Our boy," Fletcher had called Kip.

What a wonderful father Fletcher would be, Nancy

mused. Whatever he did in life, he gave it his all. His children would reap the rewards of that drive and determination . . . and so would his wife.

Wife. Children. A home. Those were some of the dreams she and Fletcher had weaved at Fletcher's Pond during that long-ago summer. Such beautiful scenarios they had created as they'd lain in the grass, sated and contented after their exquisite lovemaking. Oh, the plans they'd had for their future together. How very much in love they had been.

And still were.

Fletcher loved her, Nancy knew that now. And she loved him. But she wouldn't be his wife. There would be no home ringing with children's laughter. Their dreams had been shattered by Fletcher's restlessness, his wanderlust.

Nancy suddenly recalled what Fletcher had said about his father, and looked quickly at him. He was totally engrossed in the last minutes of the game and was apparently unaware that she was no longer screaming her head off at the umpire.

Dennis McGill, Nancy thought, had accepted Fletcher without any explanations about where he'd been, what he'd done, or what his future plans were. Dennis McGill had reached out to his son with love and welcomed him home, no questions asked.

She hadn't done that. She'd pushed aside her love for Fletcher, and used her hurt feelings and sense of betrayal as a shield, a wall of protection, against him and his overwhelming magnetism. *She* would not welcome Fletcher home with open arms. She wanted to know where he'd been, what he'd done. Why? So that she could pass judgment on him? Decide he just didn't measure up to her standards, reaffirm that he'd no doubt disappear again when the mood struck? Then she could go to Atlanta with a clear conscience, justified in her actions. She would not be guilty of what Kip had said; she wouldn't be the one now leaving Fletcher because he'd left her, and wouldn't tell her what had kept him away. He hadn't told his own father. Why should he tell her, someone who refused to tell *him* that she still loved him? Instead she keep informing him that his feelings for her were of no importance, and that she was leaving Oakville and him forever.

Oh, Lord, she thought frantically. She was so confused, so terribly muddled, she couldn't think straight about anything. She had to calm down, sort things through and—

"All right!" Fletcher shouted. "We won!" Nancy jerked in surprise, and pulled her thoughts back to where she was supposed to be. "How about a pizza to celebrate, Nance?"

"No, I—" she started to say. Would Fletcher come into clearer focus, would she know who he really was now, if she talked to him? Talked and listened, really listened? "Yes, that sounds great. Kip will be going out with his friends, and a pizza has much more appeal than the peanut butter sandwich I'd end up having."

"Then let's do it," Fletcher said, getting to his feet. "Provided I can get down out of these bleachers with this cast without killing myself. "I saw you and just hobbled up here. I didn't realize we were this high. See what you do to my brain? A man with a cast has no business climbing these rickety things. Brother."

Tit for tat, Nancy thought dryly. *Her* brain was

turning into mushy oatmeal, thanks to one Mr. Fletcher McGill.

The parking lot of the pizza parlor was full of cars. Fletcher found a spot along the street about a half a block away, then assisted Nancy out of the car. They had chatted about the game during the short drive from the high school, but fell silent as they strolled along the sidewalk.

"You know," Fletcher said finally, "I just realized that this is the first time I've taken you out to eat. That calls for a celebration at a fancy restaurant, complete with champagne."

"I love pizza," Nancy said, smiling up at him.

"The fact remains, Nance, that during our summer we never really dated like other people. We went for long drives out of town, or spent our time at Fletcher's Pond. Does it bother you that people are going to see us together?"

She stopped. "Fletcher, what a ridiculous thing to say."

"Come on," he said, taking her hand. They started off again. "I just thought I'd mention it. Tongues will wag once we're seen together."

"I don't care."

"Why? Because you're leaving Oakville anyway?"

"That has nothing to do with it. Darn it, Fletcher, what's with you? You're acting as though our being together is scandalous. The only reason we sneaked around that summer was because of the attitudes of our fathers. I make my own decisions now, and I've decided to have pizza with Fletcher McGill. It's nobody's business what we do. Or are *you* concerned about what they'll think?"

"Of course not."

"Then put a cork in it, McGill. Such nonsense."

Everything she said had been music to his ears, Fletcher thought. There were no leftover feelings of guilt within Nancy from the days when they'd been forced to meet in secrecy. She was all grown-up, knew her own mind, made her own choices.

It was time, he mused, for pizza and movies and dates to the ice cream parlor. Long overdue, in fact. They needed to go out together and learn about each other as normal couples did. It was time, but time was his enemy. He'd just have to speed things up a bit, make Nancy realize that they had everything in the world going for them. Including love.

When they entered the packed restaurant, Fletcher slipped his arm around Nancy's shoulders as they scanned the area for a table. A few people called and waved to them, then leaned forward to say something to others at their table. More heads turned in their direction.

Nancy laughed. "I feel like a goldfish in a bowl."

"They're having a great time," Fletcher said, smiling at her. "Want me to plant a whopper of a kiss on you to totally make their day?"

"I'll pass. Do you see a table?"

"Nope. How do you feel about a hamburger?"

"That's fine."

With a final wave and a smile for the very interested crowd, Fletcher escorted Nancy back out the door, pulling her close to his side in the process. And keeping her there as they walked back to the car. She made no attempt to move away.

"When do you get your cast off?" she asked.

"In a couple of weeks. This is the last stage of it. I was in the hospital for a while after surgery, but the end is in sight. I'll need some therapy to strengthen it after the cast is off, but it'll be fine. I came out of it better than the Jeep. My driver walked away without a scratch."

"He couldn't have been a very good driver if he was about to go over a cliff."

"It wasn't his fault. I insisted on going into that area, and there weren't any real roads. There'd been a lot of rain, we just slid down a muddy hill, and the rest is history."

"Oh," Nancy said. She wouldn't push it. If he wanted to tell her more, he'd tell her more. She might faint dead away from curiosity, but she wasn't going to ask.

She wasn't going to ask, Fletcher realized. That was fantastic! She seemed to sense he'd said all he cared to, and she wasn't going to hammer at him. *Thank you, Nance,* he whispered in his mind. *I love you.*

The hamburger place was also crowded, and Fletcher crossed his arms over the steering wheel and looked out the front window of the car.

"Baseball sure does wonders for appetites," he said.

"The drive-through isn't busy. Why don't we take our dinner back to my house?"

"Sold."

A short time later they were entering Nancy's living room.

"Good thing this is a small town," Fletcher said. "If we'd had a longer drive you'd have eaten all the French fries. Get your hand out of that sack, lady."

"Oh, here, fussbudget," she said, lifting out one French fry and holding it up to him. Oh, dear Lord, she thought, there was nothing sensuous—Was she listening to herself?—about feeding a French fry to a man. Unless that man was Fletcher.

Their eyes met. Fletcher caught her wrist with his hand. His white, gleaming teeth closed over the potato, and his lips followed, his gaze never leaving hers. He chewed, swallowed, then flicked his tongue between her thumb and forefinger to bring the remaining half of the fry into his mouth. Nancy's knees began to tremble, and the wild thudding of her heart echoed in her ears.

"Good," he said, his voice low and husky. "So-o-o good."

"Yes," she said, in a little puff of air. "Good."

"You turn me inside out just looking at me, Nance. What you can do with a French fry should be against the law."

"I . . . um . . ." She swallowed. "We'd better eat before it gets cold."

"Yeah."

Neither moved.

"I love you, Nance," Fletcher said.

"I know," she said in a whisper. "I know you do, Fletcher."

"Oh, Nancy." He took the bag of food from her and set it on the end table, then framed her face in his hands. He visually traced her features, one by one, then looked deep into her eyes. "Say it again," he said, his voice vibrant with emotion. "Say that you believe that I love you, that I never stopped loving you. Please, Nancy, let me hear you say it again."

"I do believe you, Fletcher."

He squeezed his eyes tightly closed for a moment, then looked at her once more. "Thank God."

"But, Fletcher, I—"

"No, no," he interrupted quickly, "don't. Don't say 'but.' Don't ruin this moment. I know we have a long way to go, but give me this moment, Nance." He lowered his head toward hers. "Please."

His lips feathered over hers, back and forth, creating a liquid fire of want and need that swirled within Nancy. His mouth was sweet torture, but she had to have more. She sank her hands into his thick, sun-streaked hair and pulled him to her, forcing his mouth hard onto hers. Their tongues met, and a groan rumbled up from Fletcher's chest.

He dropped his hands to her back, then slid them lower to cup her buttocks, nestling her in the cradle of his hips. His arousal was heavy against her.

The kiss became urgent, frenzied, hungry. Their breathing was labored in the quiet room.

They remembered the first time they had made love. The last time. And all the glorious times in between. They remembered . . . and they wanted.

Fletcher trailed his lips down Nancy's throat. Her eyes were closed, and she tilted her head back to savor the heated sensations coursing through her. She clung to his upper arms for support as he raised shaking hands to unbutton her blouse. He pulled the blouse free of her linen slacks and pushed it open, his mouth claiming a straining bud of one breast through the filmy material of her bra.

"Oh, Fletcher," she whispered, awash with shattering pleasure.

He slid his hands upward to cup her breasts. "I

want you so much," he said hoarsely. "I ache for you, Nance."

And *she* wanted *him*, Nancy thought hazily. Oh, how she wanted to be one with Fletcher.

It was too soon, her mind warned her.

Too soon? her heart asked. She'd been waiting six long years to feel this way again, to be this alive again, to make love with Fletcher again.

But who was Fletcher? her mind asked. Who had he become? Where had he been? What had he done?

It didn't matter! her heart answered. She loved him. She'd always loved him. The future, her plans . . . everything was becoming jumbled and confused. But she wanted him, that much was clear. She wanted him.

"Nancy?"

"Yes," she said, opening her eyes to gaze into his deep brown ones. "Yes, I want you, Fletcher. I need you. Once more. But not here. Kip might come home. We'll go to Fletcher's Pond. It will be just like it was before. We won't think about anything. It will be a stolen moment. Ours. Once more."

Fletcher frowned and pulled her blouse together to cover her breasts. "Once more?" he repeated. "Meaning what? Just exactly what are you saying, Nance?"

"I—I want you."

He took a step backward and narrowed his eyes. "Once more? As in, one time, one quick roll in the grass for old time's sake?"

"What an awful thing to say."

"Hey," he said, holding up his hands, "I'm just trying to make sure I understand the setup. That's it, isn't it? Once more? One time? Then what, Nance?

You go tooling off to Atlanta and the oodles of men? You'll leave, knowing that I love you?"

"Dammit, Fletcher, you left, knowing that *I* loved *you*!" she yelled. Oh, no, she hadn't meant to say that. It sounded as though she were evening the score, punishing him, making him pay a price for what had happened six years before. No, no, she hadn't meant it like that.

A shadow of pain crossed Fletcher's face and settled in the dark pools of his eyes. "I see," he said flatly. "This is a vendetta."

"No." She shook her head as tears filled her eyes.

His hands shot out and gripped her upper arms. He hauled her against him, his eyes flashing with pain and anger.

"What in the hell would you call it?" he ground out. "I've bared my soul to you. I've told you over and over how much I love you, how I never stopped loving you. For what? To be used as a stud, for a one-night stand? What did you plan to do? Take notes? Decide if I'm as good as I was six years ago?"

"Oh, please, Fletcher, don't," Nancy said, tears spilling onto her cheeks. "I didn't mean to say what I did."

"Did you mean to say that you still love me? When were you going to whip that little number on me? You don't, do you? You don't love me."

"I don't know who you are!"

"Oh, I get it," he said, a bitter edge to his voice. "You want an accounting of where I've been, what I've been doing, to decide if I qualify for your love now. Well, no dice, sweetheart. You accept me as I am, standing right here in front of you, or forget it. I won't pass tests for you, Nancy. Not ever!" He dropped his hands, causing her to stagger slightly. "I'm getting out of here." He turned toward the door.

"Fletcher, wait, please," she said, nearly choking on a sob. "Try to understand. I—" The door was slammed as Fletcher left, and Nancy jerked as if she'd been hit. Moments later she heard the sports car roar to life and be driven away with a squeal of tires. "Fletcher," she whispered. "Oh, Fletcher, I love you so much."

Nancy was snapped out of her haze of misery by the sound of Kip's voice as he called good-bye to his friends. She clutched her open blouse tightly closed in her hand, then looked frantically around the room for any telltale clues as to what had just happened.

"The hamburgers," she said, seeing the bag on the end table. She snatched it up and ran into her bedroom, closing the door just as Kip came into the house.

"Nancy?" he called. "Hey, is someone in here?"

"Yes, I'm home," she yelled through the closed door. "I'm getting ready to take a bath."

"Where's your car?"

Oh, Lord, her car. "It's at the high school. Fletcher and I went for a hamburger. He—he couldn't stay long when he brought me home. I forgot about my car."

"I'll walk over and drive it back."

"Oh, Kip, would you? I'd really appreciate it."

"No problem."

"You played a great game."

"Thanks to Fletcher. I sure didn't realize that my stance was off. The coach didn't see it, either. That Fletcher is something else. And he loves you. Awesome. This is dumb, yelling through a door, Nancy. I'll go get your car. See ya."

"Okay. 'Bye. Thanks, Kip."

Nancy leaned against the door with a sigh of relief that he was gone. There she stood, the ever-so-proper big sister, with a tearstained face, an open blouse, and a sack of cold hamburgers and fries in her hand. There she stood, awash with icy misery, and already missing Fletcher. There she stood . . . alone. "Oh, dear heaven, what am I going to do?" she said to the silence, and the tears started again.

Fletcher drove, not caring where he was going, his hands gripping the steering wheel with such force that his knuckles were white. The scene in Nancy's living room played over and over in his mind like a bad movie, causing a pain as sharp as a knife twisting in his gut.

Once more.

The words echoed and taunted him. Nancy had wanted to make love with him, be with him, just once more. He now knew that she believed him when he told her that he loved her. The rush of relief, of pure joy, that had swept through him when she'd admitted she believed him had been incredible.

But then she had picked up the pieces of the past and hurled them at him, cutting him to the quick with their jagged edges.

And with the truth.

"Damn," Fletcher said, pounding the steering wheel with his fist. He *had* left her, knowing how deeply she loved him.

During those six years the hot-tempered, reckless

boy had changed into the man he was now. He still had a temper, he conceded, but he was different now, and that was what he had wanted Nance to see.

He had seen the changes in her, too, recognized and respected the woman she had become. She was stronger, a woman of courage and determination, one who knew her own mind. And he loved her even more than when she had been the essence of innocence, coming to him at Fletcher's Pond in total trust, so giving.

But now she had said she didn't know him at all. Dammit, did that really mean she didn't love him anymore? That wasn't true, was it?

Why could he see her so clearly, yet she couldn't see him? Why was he so sure of his love for her, and that she was running from her feelings for him? Why was he dreaming of a lifetime with her, when all she wanted was "once more" before she left him?

"I don't know who you are!"

Nancy's words and his harshly spoken reply came quickly to mind.

"I won't pass tests for you, Nancy. Not ever!"

But, he thought suddenly, hadn't she passed tests for him? Subtly, quietly, the past six years of her life had been spread before him for his inspection. He'd simply gone to Fletcher's Pond, and there she'd been, as though she'd been waiting for him. The only piece missing was her possible involvement with other men, and he'd cleverly gained that information. She was his Nance; older, more confident, but possessing the same values and conducting herself with dignity and class. She was warm and giving, and he had to believe that she still loved him.

"I don't know who you are!"

Lord, he thought, running a shaking hand over the back of his neck. She didn't! She didn't know who he was, who he'd become. He'd wanted her to see for herself the changes in him, accept him as the man he now was. But his life was clouded in the mystery he refused to reveal, and wasn't spread before her as her life had been for him.

Six years ago, he mused, he'd said that he loved her. Six years ago he'd left her. Now he was back, declaring his love. Was she waiting for the good-bye again, protecting herself from the heartache she fully expected to suffer when he packed up and left?

And in spite of that, she had been willing to make love with him . . . once more.

Good Lord, he thought. What had he done? It had been so clear in his mind. He desperately needed Nancy to accept him as the man he now was. But how could she do that when he wouldn't tell her anything about himself? What was there for her to see, except that he was back, telling her that he loved her? She had no reason to believe he wouldn't repeat his disappearing act of six years ago.

He'd expected too much of her, he realized, asked far, far too much. He was such a fool, he told himself. Such an arrogant, cocky fool. He'd had it all planned out so perfectly once he'd discovered she was still in Oakville. He and Nancy would pick up where they'd left off, nurture their love once again, look to a future together. Then, without its having influenced her decision in any way, he'd tell her all she had the right to know about the six-year gap in his life.

Why? he wondered. Why had it been so important to him that it be done in that order? Why?

Because he was afraid.

Big time, strutting-his-stuff Fletcher McGill was afraid. He wanted Nancy to love him just for himself, as she had so long ago. He didn't want her swayed by the truth of what he'd done. The icy chill of fear had blurred his judgment, caused him to have niggling doubts about Nancy's inner self, the woman she'd become, doubts about the sincerity and depth of her love for him, should she declare it *after* she knew the truth.

Damn his insecurities, Fletcher thought, fuming. A part of him, deep inside, was still a boy, not a man. The same boy who had sought acceptance by the other high-school athletes, had silently begged them to forget he was a McGill, forget he had money, just see him as one of them. And they had. Then, later, Nancy had accepted him, pushed aside the facts of who he was and simply loved him.

That was what he'd wanted from her again, he knew, but this time there were six years missing. This time there were protective walls built around Nance's heart. Walls she had built with the bricks created by the pain and tears he'd caused her. Oh, yes, he could see it all now so clearly. And, oh, hell, yes, he was asking far too much of her.

"I don't know who you are!"

No, Fletcher thought wearily, she didn't.

The same fear that clutched his heart held a viselike grip on his ability to tell her the truth. The consuming need from his childhood to be accepted just for himself had followed him into his manhood.

It was his demon, his nemesis, and he had to conquer it.

His eyes widened as he saw the skyline of Atlanta in the distance, pulling him from his tormented thoughts. He'd driven nearly two hours without even being aware of it. He checked the traffic, then crossed the divider in the highway at the next opening.

He slowed his speed and headed back in the direction from which he'd come. He was going home, to Oakville. Wiser, and with a greater understanding of himself, he was going home.

And with every passing mile, the chill of fear within him grew.

Six

For Nancy, the next day at work was a study in frustration. She hadn't slept well, her head ached, and she made numerous silly errors. To add to her generally rotten mood, the majority of the patients visiting Dr. Lansing had a comment to make regarding Nancy and Fletcher's being together the previous evening. While most of the people spoke favorably of the surprising twosome, Nancy was in no frame of mind to have to force a smile continually and say something polite but noncommittal.

"Well," June said to Nancy in the middle of the afternoon, "aren't you the celebrity today? I didn't even realize you knew Fletcher McGill."

"People are making a federal case out of seeing us at the pizza parlor. We didn't even stay, because it was too crowded."

"Ah, yes, but there's also the kiss at the baseball game," June said, wiggling her eyebrows. "I may be sixty-two, but I'm not dead. I wouldn't mind one iota if that Fletcher McGill kissed me at a baseball game. Actually, though, I think I'd hold out for a more romantic setting."

"June, for heaven's sake, it wasn't a kiss, as in 'kiss.' Kip had just hit a home run, and we were excited, and—Oh, forget it. I have work to do."

June's laughter followed Nancy as she escaped to her tiny office and tried once again to post correctly the patients' charges of the day to the proper accounts.

No, Nancy thought dryly, the baseball kiss hadn't been a kiss, as in "kiss." But later, in her living room, those had been kisses! The mere remembrance of Fletcher's mouth claiming hers, the rugged length of his body pressed to hers, his taste, his aroma, brought a flush to her cheeks and desire thrumming deep within her.

Once more.

The words she had spoken had caused Fletcher to rage in anger, to accuse her of so many things that still hurt when she thought of them. She was drowning, Nancy realized, in a churning sea of confusion. She was being swept away on a tidal wave of emotions that centered on Fletcher, who loved her, but not enough to tell her where he'd been.

It wasn't a test she was putting him through, she told herself. It wasn't! She loved him. It was as simple and as complicated as that. She loved him, and because she did, she wanted and needed to know him. His secrets, his refusal to share the unknown portions of his life with her, the missing six years, brought an ache to her heart and tears to her eyes.

What was she going to do? she wondered. She

could feel herself slipping into a place where nothing mattered but Fletcher; not her plans or her pride, or anything. That was wrong, so very wrong. She wasn't an eighteen-year-old child; she was a woman who wanted to be an equal partner in a relationship with her man.

An equal partner?

Nancy sat bolt upright in her chair, her eyes wide. There she was, she realized, feeling sorry for herself because Fletcher was keeping secrets from her, wasn't meeting her halfway. Yet she had been keeping from him the most important message of all.

She hadn't told him that she still loved him!

Dear heaven, she thought, sinking back in her chair. She expected Fletcher to tell her things he hadn't told his own father. Who in the blue blazes did she think she was?

It *would* appear as though she were testing him, she admitted. If what he'd done for the past six years met her approval, he would have the honor of hearing her declare her love for him. She could see it so clearly now through Fletcher's eyes, and it didn't paint a very pretty picture of her.

But it wasn't like that, she inwardly argued, not really, not quite. The past was important because it could very well hold the key to Fletcher's plans for the future. A future in which maybe, just maybe, he intended to include her. Instead of dwelling on where he had been, her thoughts should have been centered on where he was going, what he wanted from tomorrow. But if the past and the future were tied together, why should he tell her?

She'd never told him that she still loved him. She'd been holding her heart in reserve, she now knew, protecting herself against more heartache. Well, it was too late for all of that. She loved Fletcher with an intensity beyond description. To tell him of that love, then have him leave her once again, wasn't going to increase her pain and loneliness, make it worse than if she'd never said the words to him. She was a lost cause, a woman in love with a man who could ride off into the sunset tomorrow and never look back.

There was a glimmer of hope, she thought, that Fletcher was waiting, hoping, praying to hear her declaration of love. There was a slim chance that that was what it would take to unlock the secrets within him and have him tell her of the past six years, and of the plans he had for the six times six years ahead.

"I'll tell him," Nancy said softly to the empty room. "I'll tell him that I love him."

The remainder of the afternoon dragged by. At five o'clock Nancy forced one more smile as she bid June good-bye, and left the office.

Fletcher's car was parked right in front of the office, and he was leaning against it. Nancy stopped abruptly when she saw him, and blinked.

"Hi," Fletcher said quietly.

She swallowed. "Hello."

"I'd like to talk to you, but I don't have much time. Could we go for a drive?"

"Well, I . . . Yes, of course. You don't have much time?"

"Come on," he said, opening the car door for her.

Nancy's trembling legs managed to get her across the sidewalk, and she sank gratefully into the plush seat of the car. Fletcher slid behind the wheel, started the ignition, and pulled away from the curb. Three people stopped on the sidewalk to stare after them.

"Did you have a rough day?" Fletcher asked, glancing over at her. "You know, with people having things to say about our being together?"

"It doesn't matter. It wasn't any more than I expected. Fletcher, I'm sorry about what happened at my house last night. I've thought about it all day, and all night, really, and I—"

"No," he interrupted, "I'm the one who's sorry. I drove for hours last night, sorting things through, and it became clear to me."

"What did?"

He drove in silence for several minutes. At the edge of town he turned onto a narrow dirt road that cut through the woods. He shut off the ignition, then shifted in his seat to face her.

"No one will see us here, Nance. I'd rather go to Fletcher's Pond with you, but I don't have time."

"You keep saying that," she said, also turning to face him. "Do you have to be someplace?"

"Atlanta. I have a plane to catch."

No! she screamed silently. Oh, no. He was leaving. He was leaving her . . . again. Not now, not yet. Oh, please, no. She hadn't told him that she loved him, she hadn't had the chance to fight for him, see if her love could make a difference. Oh, Fletcher, please. No.

"Plane," she said dully, feeling the color drain from her face. "You have a plane to catch in Atlanta."

"Yes."

"You're leaving." Oh dear Lord, it hurt. She couldn't do this. She couldn't sit there and hear those words.

She wanted to run, just get out of that car and run as fast as she could.

"Nance, listen to me. Nancy?"

"What?" she asked. Her heart hurt. It was pounding in her chest, and it hurt. It was shattering into a million pieces, and it hurt so very much.

Fletcher reached across the gear shift and gripped her shoulders, giving her a small shake, a deep frown on his face.

"Nance, please," he said. "You're not with me. You look like you're a million miles away. You've got to listen to me."

"Yes," she said, taking a deep breath, "I'm listening."

"Okay. Look, I know I don't have the right to ask this of you, but I'm going to do it anyway. I realize I've done nothing to make you trust me, but that's what I'm asking of you. Trust me, Nance. I'm flying to New York tonight. I'll be back in Atlanta on Saturday. I want you to meet me in Atlanta then. I'll have a room registered in your name at the Hilton. Will you do it? Will you come to Atlanta on Saturday?"

"You're . . . coming back? You're going to New York, then coming back?"

"Yes."

"But—"

"No, please, don't start asking questions, because I have to go. Just tell me you'll be in that hotel on Saturday."

"But—"

"Nance, please," he said, a frantic edge to his voice.

He pulled her to him, and his mouth melted over

hers, his questing tongue meeting hers in a kiss that seemed to steal the very breath from her body. She gave way to the sensations rocketing through her as she encircled his neck with her arms.

The kiss was rough, igniting the ever-smoldering embers of desire within them. Passion burst into a roaring flame of want and need.

Fletcher tore his mouth from hers. "Say you'll come to Atlanta Saturday," he said, his breathing labored. "You'll have your own room. You're not agreeing to make love with me. I just need you to be there. Trust me, Nance. You have no reason to, but that's what I'm asking of you. Please."

She had no choice, Nancy thought foggily. She loved him. She loved him, and she wanted him to know that she did.

"Fletcher, I—"

"Yes or no? Will you come?"

"Yes."

"Thank you," he said, so softly, she hardly heard him.

He shifted back behind the wheel and turned the key in the ignition, backing the car out from beneath the branches of the trees in the next instant.

"Fletcher, I want to tell you—"

"Nance," he interrupted, glancing at her quickly, "don't say anything else, okay? I have your word that you'll be there Saturday. Leave it at that for now. Do this my way, all right? Just trust me."

She nodded, unable to speak as her mind whirled with unanswered questions and her body hummed with heated desire.

A few minutes later Fletcher pulled up in front of

the dentist's office. He reached over and trailed his thumb over her lips.

"Saturday."

"Saturday," she said, feeling like a mechanical robot. "The Hilton. Atlanta."

"Just wait for me in your room."

"Yes."

"Thank you, Nance."

"Yes," she said, then opened the car door, wondering absently if her wobbly legs were going to support her.

She stepped out onto the sidewalk and watched as Fletcher drove away above the speed limit. She continued just to stand there, hardly able to breathe, totally incapable of thinking clearly.

"So that's how it is," a deep voice said.

Nancy snapped out of her trance and looked up to see Brad standing next to her.

"What?" she asked.

"You and Fletch. I've been hearing gossip at the bank all day about you two, and now I've seen it for myself. Why didn't you tell me, Nancy?"

"You don't understand. It's very complicated and—"

"And none of my business, really. You never played games with me. You were always honest about your feelings toward me. I just didn't know Fletch was in the picture. I like him, Nancy, you know that. But be careful, okay? I don't want to see you get hurt. Fletch has been gone a long time. He seems to be a decent guy, but—Well, there's a helluva lot of secrecy surrounding him as to where he's been and what he's been doing."

"Yes, I know," she said softly.

"I'll be around if you need me, Nancy."

"Oh, Brad, I'm sorry. I never meant to hurt you. There's so much you don't know, and I can't explain it. I'm so sorry."

"Hey, it's not your fault. I knew where I stood with you. I was dreaming we could make it, that's all. Fletcher McGill is a lucky man, and I hope he realizes it. Please, Nancy, just be careful. I'll see you." Brad hurried away.

Feeling numb and totally exhausted, Nancy drove home and entered the small, quiet house. A note from Kip that was held on the refrigerator door by a magnet shaped like a baseball bat said that he was eating dinner at Bernie's, then studying there for an exam. Nancy opened the refrigerator, stared at the contents, then closed it again. She sank into a chair at the table, suddenly remembering Kip's words spoken there days before. Words that had turned her world upside down.

"Fletcher McGill is back."

Yes, she mused, Fletcher McGill was back. And her life would never be the same again.

She was actually driving to Atlanta on Saturday, checking into the Hilton, then waiting for Fletcher. She was actually going to do that! Unbelievable. She didn't even know why Fletcher wanted her there, but she was going, no questions asked. Not, she reasoned, that he'd given her an opportunity to ask any questions. Trust him, he'd said, and she'd bobbed her little head up and down, agreeing to his mysterious request. Now she was left facing the task of explaining to her impressionable young brother why she was doing such an asinine thing.

And left trying to explain it to herself.

No, that wasn't true, she admitted. She knew why

she'd agreed to go to Atlanta. It was so simple, it was ridiculous. Fletcher had asked her to.

"Oh, my," Nancy said aloud, pressing her hands to her cheeks. How was she going to survive the next few days, the waiting and wondering about what was to transpire in Atlanta? She'd be a basket case by then, a blithering idiot, a—

"Nancy!"

"Aagh!" she screamed, jumping in her chair.

"Just me," Kip said, striding into the kitchen. "Bernie doesn't feel well, so I came on home. What's doing?"

"I'm going to Atlanta Saturday to meet Fletcher," Nancy blurted out in a rush of words. "I'll stay overnight, I guess, but I'll have my own room. I don't know why I'm going. I mean, I know I'm going because I love him and he asked me to go, but I don't know why he asked me to go, because he didn't tell me. He's flying to New York tonight, but I don't know why he's doing that either. Well, gosh, I sure don't know much, do I?" A rather wobbly giggle escaped from her lips. "You probably think I'm really dumb to go to Atlanta, when I don't know why I'm going. What can I say? I'm nuts. There are times when being in love is not all it's cracked up to be. But then again—"

"Whoa," Kip said, raising his hand. "You're going to run out of oxygen. Believe it or not, I caught everything you said. Want my opinion?"

"Why not?' she asked, throwing up her hands.

"Trust Fletcher."

"That's it? That's your entire donation to this screwy mess?"

"Yep."

"Thanks for nothing."

"No problem. It's all part of my job as man of the family." He opened the refrigerator and took out two apples and an orange. "I'll have an orgy while you're gone."

" 'Kay," Nancy said absently, staring off into space.

Kip laughed, shook his head, and left the room. It was another hour before Nancy moved.

Thursday and Friday dragged by even more slowly than Nancy would have thought possible. Her mood swings were extreme. She bounced back and forth between wanting to fling herself into Fletcher's arms and wanting to punch him right in his gorgeous nose. Kip spent a great deal of time grinning at her, which earned him endless stormy glares. At night Nancy tossed and turned, then dreamed of Fletcher when she finally managed to sleep.

At last Saturday morning arrived, and Nancy stood staring into the empty suitcase she'd set on her bed, realizing she had no idea what to pack.

That wasn't her fault, she reasoned. When a person didn't know why she was going on the trip she was going on, she could hardly be expected to know what to take with her.

"A little of this, a little of that," she said breezily, tossing in some bikini panties. "I'm hysterical. I know I am. I'm over the edge. I'm going to strangle Fletcher."

Dressed in burgundy-colored slacks and a soft, rose-colored blouse, Nancy reread the list of instructions she'd left for Kip, took a deep breath, and walked out the front door. She was past wondering how there was room within her for all the emotions she was experiencing: excitement, fear, doubt, love, even a little anger. They were all there, tumbling together.

The only thing that was crystal-clear was that whatever took place in Atlanta was going to change her life forever. She knew that. Somehow she just knew that.

Nancy's room at the Hilton was actually a suite, which included a spacious living room. She'd never been in such fancy surroundings, and wandered around looking at everything with a sense of awe.

There had been no messages waiting for her at the front desk, so she'd simply checked in, unpacked, then wondered where Fletcher was. They hadn't set an exact time to meet, she realized, so all she could do was be patient.

At two she went to the coffee shop for lunch, sitting at a table where she could see the front entrance to the hotel. By three she was back in her room.

Pacing.

No Fletcher.

Four o'clock.

No Fletcher.

By five o'clock Nancy's nerves were stretched to the breaking point.

When a knock sounded at the door at five-twenty, she gasped and placed her hand on her heart. After two deep, steadying breaths she went to the door and opened it.

"I'm sorry I'm so late," Fletcher said without an

actual greeting. He stepped into the room, closed the door, pulled her into his arms, and kissed her.

Hello, Fletcher, she thought dreamily as she returned the passionate kiss in total abandon.

"I missed you," he said close to her lips when he finally ended the searing embrace. "I was also scared to death you wouldn't come."

"I said I would," she replied breathlessly.

"Yeah, well, you had a couple of days to think it over. But you're here, and I thank you." He set her gently away from him. "Is the room all right?"

"It's beautiful. I don't need a whole suite."

"Yes, you do. You deserve the best there is."

"Thank you. Fletcher, you look tired."

"It's been a very hectic few days. In fact, I have to leave you now for a while. I'll pick you up at seven for dinner. Did you bring a fancy dress? You know, something slinky?"

"Yes, I packed a variety of things, because I didn't know what to expect."

"Good. Wear the slinky."

"Fletcher, aren't you going to tell me why I'm here?"

"You're here because I love you." He gave her a quick kiss. "I'll be back at seven. 'Bye," he said, and left the room.

"I love you too," she said, frowning at the closed door. "I have, however, had just about enough of this cloak-and-dagger jazz, Mr. McGill."

Nancy's dress was the color of a peach that was ready to be plucked from a tree. Made of chiffon, it had a straight skirt that fell to just above her ankles, with a petal hem and a dramatic tunic top that left one shoulder entirely bare. Nancy had never been able to decide if she looked utterly smashing in the creation, or like an ordinary dish of peach yogurt.

If the expression on Fletcher's face when he arrived at seven was any indication, Nancy looked smashing. While she stared at him, he stared at her.

"You're beautiful," he said, his voice hushed.

"So are you," she said. "I've never seen you in a tuxedo. My goodness, Fletcher, you're . . . you're stunning."

He chuckled. "Especially with the cast."

Stunning, Nancy repeated to herself. The tuxedo was very expensive, obviously custom-made, and fit Fletcher to perfection. His shoulders looked so wide, his hips narrow, thighs muscled. The tiny pleats on his pristine white shirt did nothing to diminish his masculinity. If he heard the wild thudding of her heart, she'd absolutely die of embarrassment.

"Shall we go?" Fletcher asked. Lord above, she was sensational, he thought. He wanted to haul her into his arms and hold her close, feel the lush material of that dress beneath his hands as it moved over her soft skin. He wanted to crush her to him, to mold her feminine curves to his body. He wanted . . . Hell, he just plain wanted her, all of her, wanted to make love to her. Now. "*Now!* I mean, now we should go to dinner. We're on a tight schedule."

"All right." Nancy picked up a lacy peach-colored shawl and her clutch purse, and preceded Fletcher out the door.

As she brushed past him, he inhaled her light perfume and inwardly groaned. The very essence of Nance was driving him nuts. That, along with the knot in his stomach caused by the evening ahead, added up to a dying man.

Nancy turned in the hallway and smiled at him.

But what a way to go, Fletcher thought. Fletcher McGill would check out with a foolish grin on his face.

Fletcher had made reservations at an exclusive restaurant in Atlanta, and they were led to a cozy table. He selected, tasted, and approved the wine, then lifted his glass in a toast.

"To Fletcher's Pond," he said. "Where it all began."

Nancy lifted her glass but said nothing before taking a sip. They ordered their dinners, their salads arrived, and still neither of them had spoken further.

"Nancy," Fletcher said finally, "I appreciate your not badgering me with all the questions I know you must have. Everything will become clear to you very soon."

"Yes, I do have questions, Fletcher, but I've come this far, so I'll just wait, I guess."

"Thank you." He paused. "Do you remember when we used to lie in the grass at Fletcher's Pond making plans for the future, our future?"

"Yes," she said softly.

"Do you realize how much fantasizing we did? We'd live on a yacht, or in a castle in Spain. We'd have a different house for every season of the year."

"They were silly dreams; we knew that. We were just having fun."

"Yeah, but we never got around to really planning something realistic. I had a business degree that I was supposed to use at the mill until the day I retired, and you were going to get some skills at the business school here in Atlanta."

"I'm a very good bookkeeper without having been able to take all the classes. It's not a great job, but it's steady. My real challenge has been in the computer field, though. I had to learn it on my own, and it has given me a great sense of accomplishment. As far as these past years have gone, I've liked my work."

"You're lucky. I hated what I did at the mill."

"I know you did."

"The thing is, Nancy, I wasn't trained to do anything else. I was good in sports, but I missed my chance at that. When I left Oakville that night six years ago, I didn't know where I was going or what I was going to do. You were right not to come with me. I nearly starved for a while."

"You had money in the Oakville bank."

"I made up my mind I wasn't going to touch it. Not a penny. It was a matter of honor. I was walking away from the McGills and the McGill way of life. I decided I had no right to the McGill money, either. I signed on as a crewman on an oil tanker down the coast. I discovered very quickly what hard labor was all about. I did all kinds of jobs for the first six months, in all kinds of places. I was experiencing life for the first time. And through it all, Nance, I thought about you."

"Your dinner," the waiter said, hovering at Nancy's elbow.

Fletcher waited until their food had been served and the waiter had moved away.

"Nancy," he continued, "it became very clear to me that I had a long way to go as far as learning responsibility and being a worthwhile man—not a boy, a man—were concerned. I knew I was going to lose you by staying away, but I had nothing to offer you if I came home."

"Oh, Fletcher, that's not true. You gave me so much that summer."

"But not enough," he said, leaning toward her. "I'm not talking about material things. Nance, I left you, and as far as I knew you were lost to me forever. I had no one but myself left. I made up my mind to become a respectable man in my own right. Not a McGill, per se, just me. That's what . . ." He paused and frowned.

"Go on, Fletcher," Nancy urged gently.

"That's what I'd been struggling for all of my life . . . to be accepted for myself, for who I was. I managed it in high school because of the sports. I had it again that summer with you. But the rest of the time? I was a McGill first, *then* Fletcher, the person. Lord, I hated that. It's a frightening feeling wondering whether people are coming on to you for yourself or because you're a McGill and you have something they want."

"Yes," Nancy said, nodding slowly, "I understand. I wish you'd explained all this to me that summer, Fletcher. I had no idea it meant so very much to you."

"I didn't get a real handle on it myself until I went away. I figured that it was a trade-off. I'd lost you, but I was going to gain me, myself. There were times when I missed you so much, ached for you, was so damn lonely, that I decided I had screwed up my entire life. But, then, slowly, it started to come together for me."

"What did? Where did you go? You discovered

who you are, what you were meant to do? Can't you tell me now, Fletcher?"

Dammit, he thought, frustrated. Couldn't she say it first, tell him that she loved him? Couldn't she give him that now, before he spread his life out in front of her? The old fears, his demons, were twisting inside of him. Didn't she understand how desperately he needed to hear her declaration of love *now?*

"Your dinner is getting cold," he said, his voice raspy. "You'd better eat, because we don't have much time."

"Much time before what?"

"Before you get all your answers," he said, a muscle ticking in his jaw.

Nancy directed her attention to her meal, forcing herself to eat, though she didn't taste a thing. There had been a flicker of pain in Fletcher's eyes, she thought frantically, and she'd caused it, somehow. He was so tense, he could hardly sit still, and he was trying so hard to make things clear to her. She understood what he'd been trying to say. She saw his need to be accepted for himself, not as just another one of the McGills. She'd told him she understood, yet somehow she'd failed him in the past few minutes.

Oh, how she ached to tell him that she loved him, she thought. But it would be selfish to blurt it out now. This was Fletcher's night. He was opening himself up to her, was prepared to show her all he had become. She couldn't brush that aside by saying, "That's all very fascinating, Fletcher, but now let me tell you how *I* feel. I love you." No, this wasn't the time. He was doing this his way, and she loved him enough to be patient and wait.

They finished the meal in silence.

"We'd better go," Fletcher said, signaling to the waiter.

Go where? Nancy wondered frantically, but all she said was, "Yes, all right."

He looked at her for a long moment, searching her face, gazing deep into her eyes. Then he sighed, got to his feet and extended his hand to her.

Seven

Darkness had settled, and with it came a multitude of twinkling stars, but Nancy didn't notice. The aroma of spring flowers wafted through the air, fragrant enough to mask the odor of exhaust fumes from the heavy traffic, but Nancy didn't notice. Atlanta was alive with the excitement of Saturday night— glittering lights, boisterous people, activities of all kinds to choose from, but Nancy didn't notice.

As Fletcher drove, she glanced over at him often, fighting back the irrational urge to beg him to turn the car around and head for Oakville. She was suddenly terribly frightened at the thought of what she was about to discover concerning Fletcher. The missing six years of his life were going to be revealed to her, the secrets gone, the mystery solved. Who and what Fletcher now was would be presented to her for her inspection.

And she was scared to death.

Why, she asked herself, would her Fletcher of Fletcher's Pond, her loving, tender, reckless Fletcher, need the trappings of this city, the finery of a tuxedo and her own peach-colored dress, as a backdrop for his moment of truth? Who was he?

"Trust me, Nance," Fletcher said quietly. "I can feel how tense you are. I could try to explain all this to you, but it's better that you see for yourself. We won't stay long, and I'll be with you every minute. Trust me."

She nodded as she clenched her hands tightly in her lap. Trust him, she thought. Of course she trusted him, because she loved him. But if that were true, then why were they there? Why had she put Fletcher in a position where he had to prove himself to her, as he was about to do? He was indeed passing tests for her at that very moment, probably with the hope and prayer that the evidence of his six years away from her would meet with her approval. She had no right to do this. Love wasn't conditional, scored on a sheet, with points added up to see if you qualified.

Yes, she admitted, the woman within her, the person, wanted to know where Fletcher had been and what he'd been doing. But Nance, Fletcher's Nance, his lover, his love—did she have the right to demand an accounting of six years when they'd been tied to each other only in their own hearts and minds? Oh, dear Lord, she suddenly didn't know. It was all so frightening, and so very confusing.

She had to tell him that she loved him, Nancy thought frantically. She had to tell him now, before they got to wherever it was they were going. Then . . . yes . . . then they would stand together, side by side, equal partners, two people in love. They would be united, seeing—but not judging—the missing six years.

For in that moment Nancy knew that the six years didn't matter.

What was important was the now, the moment wherein they lived and loved, and all the tomorrows to come.

"Fletcher," she said, looking over at him, "please listen to me. I want to tell you that I—"

"We're here," he interrupted. "We can talk later."

Nancy turned to see a brightly lit building that was set back off the road. A sweeping plush lawn was visible beneath the silvery luminescence of the moon and stars, and rows of expensive cars were parked in a paved lot. She saw several elegantly dressed couples approach the front doors of the building.

"What—what is this place?" she asked, her throat suddenly dry.

"You'll see." Fletcher drove to the front, where a valet immediately opened Nancy's door and assisted her from the car. Fletcher joined her and lightly gripped her elbow as they walked up the wide front stairs. Nancy's knees were trembling. "I love you," Fletcher whispered close to her ear. "Remember that."

"Yes. Yes, I will. But I want to tell you—"

"Good evening," a tuxedo-clad man said at the door. "Your invitation, sir?"

Fletcher reached inside his jacket for an engraved card and handed it to the man.

"Thank you, sir. Enjoy your evening."

She had choices, Nancy thought giddily. She could cut and run, or faint, or throw up, or quit acting like a dolt and simply walk inside that building with Fletcher.

"Ready?" Fletcher said to her.

No! "Yes."

Fletcher slid his hand to the small of her back and urged her forward. They stepped inside, and were met by the hum of voices and a crush of people. There was a buzz of excitement in the air, a festive mood, but the knot in Nancy's stomach tightened, and she had the horrible thought that the choices available to her were no longer up for a vote, and she might donate her dinner to the cause.

"What is this place, Fletcher?" she asked again, trying to ignore the precarious state of her stomach.

"Come over this way," he said, steering her through the crowd. A large embossed sign was set on an easel. "Read that."

Nancy frowned as she read the sign. "A special one-night showing, by invitation only, of the works of photographer David Forester, in cooperation with the Gallery of Fillegree, New York City. The photographs displayed may be purchased at the prices indicated in the brochure. We are honored to have Mr. Forester's work here at the MacBeth Gallery in Atlanta. Mr. Forester is known the world over for his photographs, which depict all walks of life. Since his work centers on people's faces, and he refuses to reveal his identity, Mr. Forester is often referred to as the 'Elusive Man of the Faces.' We thank him for sharing his rare gift with Atlanta, Georgia."

Nancy looked quickly at Fletcher. He was watching her, and she couldn't read the expression on his face.

"David Forester," she said. "Yes, I've heard of him. I've seen his work in magazines, and there was a special about him on 'Sixty Minutes.' I remember one photograph of a child, a little girl, in Cambodia. He won an award for it. Oh, that little girl broke my heart. She wasn't more than four years old, but she—I don't know—she seemed as though she were ancient, as though she would never laugh again, never hope or dream. I cried. I sat in front of the TV and cried. The photograph was in black and white. He does all his work in black and white. I'll never forget that little girl. The photograph was called—"

" 'Child of the Silent Eyes,' " Fletcher said quietly.

"Yes. But Fletcher, I don't understand. What does" —she glanced around—"what does all of this have to do with you?"

"Come on," he said, taking her hand.

He led her through the crowd, toward the back of the building. Nancy looked quickly at the photographs they passed, seeing the many different faces. Some were happy and bright with eagerness; others were tragically sad and empty. Faces of all ages. Faces of all races. Faces of life.

They entered a small, plushly furnished office, which was glowing with soft light from lamps on end tables flanking a velvet sofa. Fletcher closed the door, then took a deep breath as Nancy turned to face him.

"Nance," he said, his voice oddly husky, "I'm . . . I'm David Forester."

Nancy felt the color drain from her face as she took a step backward. Fletcher was David Forester? Oh, he was not. Why was he joking around at a time like this? Fletcher was David Forester? "I beg your pardon?"

"It's true, Nance."

She backed up several more steps, her eyes wide as she stared at Fletcher. She bumped into a chair and sank into it gratefully, her mind whirling from the impact of Fletcher's words.

"I . . . How . . . Why . . ." she started to ask, only to press her hands to her cheeks and shake her head. "I don't know what to say. I don't remember your ever expressing an interest in photography."

"I didn't have one," he said. He unbuttoned his jacket and shoved his hands into his pockets. "It was just a fluke. About six months after I left Oakville I won a camera in a poker game. It was a good piece of equipment, and I decided to figure out how it worked, see what I could do with it."

Nancy dropped her hands to her lap, her gaze riveted on Fletcher.

"I started out taking pictures of flowers, trees, rocks. Then I began to look at people. I was in Alaska, and I suddenly realized I was in the midst of a culture I knew nothing about. I spent time with the Eskimos, listened to them, lived with them, came to understand them."

"And took their pictures," she said softly.

"Yes. Faces. I learned to see, really see, the stories reflected in people's faces. It was a growing time for me. The cocky, self-centered kid began to change into a man. I began to reach beyond myself and realize that there was a world out there that didn't focus entirely on Fletcher McGill. Then I met a newspaper photographer who was on assignment in

Anchorage for a New York magazine. I showed him some of my stuff, and he was impressed enough to take it back to New York with him to an agent he knew. I told the newspaper guy that my name was David Forester."

"Why?" Nancy asked, leaning slightly forward.

"My old fears, Nance." He stared up at the ceiling for a long moment before looking at her again. "I had a terrible image in my mind of my photographs getting all mixed up with the McGill name and reputation. Then what would I have sold? My work, or who I was? My middle name is David."

"Yes, I know."

"The Forester was for you, Nancy, the memory of you, of what we'd shared, of how much I still loved and missed you. Forester was as close to Forest as I could risk getting without having someone possibly make the connection."

"Oh, Fletcher," she said, her eyes filling with tears.

"The agent was very charged up about the pictures. She took care of everything, and I just kept traveling around the world, seeing and finding the faces."

"Fletcher, your work is known everywhere. David Forester is highly successful. You made it on your own without using the McGill name. Why are you still being so secretive about it, refusing to step forward and say that you are David Forester?"

He drew in a shuddering breath and raked a hand through his hair. "One year just slid into the next. I became very comfortable with the arrangement. No one paid any attention to me, because David Forester had never granted an interview or been photographed. In India, in Vietnam, in Africa, no one knew who Fletcher McGill was. I was just a guy messing around with a camera for kicks. If I made friends, was welcomed into homes, it was because of me, who I was as a person, nothing more. The name David Forester became my enemy in those foreign countries as my reputation spread, so I stayed Fletcher McGill over there. It was so good, Nance, to be accepted just for myself. I needed that so damn much."

"Oh, Fletcher," she said, getting to her feet.

"Then I smashed my ankle and was laid up for what seemed like forever. I had a lot of time to think. I realized that I was really tired; physically, mentally, emotionally. It was time to come home. I didn't analyze it. I just got on a plane when I was able to and did it. And it was meant to be, don't you see, because you were still in Oakville. If I'd delayed, you'd have been gone."

A light knock at the door caused Fletcher to spin around and open it a crack. In the next instant he waved in a tall, strikingly beautiful blond woman in her thirties. Her full-length white dress clung to her voluptuous figure.

"I thought I saw you come in here," she said. "The last photograph just sold, David Fletcher. You're a smash hit in Atlanta, Georgia. Congratulations, sweetheart."

Sweetheart? Nancy thought. Who was this woman? Well, at least she hadn't called Fletcher "dah-ling," but still . . . Oh, good grief, she was gorgeous. *She* certainly didn't look like peach yogurt.

"You must be Nancy," the woman said, smiling.

"Who? Oh, yes, I am."

"Nancy Forest," Fletcher said, "meet the best agent in New York City, Selene St. Simon. Selene, this is my Nance."

"Who caused me to work my lovely tush off," Selene said, laughing. "I have never put anything together as quickly as I did this show. I had those invitations delivered by messenger, you know. David Fletcher McGill Forester, you are going to get a bill from me that you won't believe. But"—she shrugged—"it was all done in the name of true love. I adore romance. Now, remember, no slip of the tongue about who you are, or we'll get our fannies sued. You gave exclusive rights to disclosing your identity to those ever-so-generous book-publishing people. Well, I must go mingle. Great meeting you, Nancy. Hang on to this sweetheart. He's one in a million." She kissed Fletcher full on the mouth. " 'Bye love."

"I'll talk to you soon, Selene," he said, then closed the door behind her.

"I didn't know agents looked like that," Nancy said, frowning slightly.

He shrugged. "Mine does. I didn't know it either for the first couple of years, because we did everything by phone. When I finally met her, I nearly fell over. Anyway, she's a top-notch agent."

"Fletcher, she said something about a book, and about revealing your identity."

"I had to let Selene know I'd been hurt and couldn't get around for a while. I told her I needed a break from the constant travel, and she suggested a book, with me writing the text, giving background information and doing human-interest pieces on the people in the photographs. The publisher agreed only if I'd reveal my identity. He said the secrecy had gone on long enough, and speculation about who David Forester was could overshadow my work. Selene agreed with him, badgered the hell out of me by phone while I was flat on my back in the hospital, and I finally relented. I held out for having final say on which pictures go into the book. I'll dedicate it to 'Child of the Silent Eyes,' and her picture will be on the first page."

"It's a very moving picture, Fletcher."

"Yeah, well, she makes me appreciate life, and the fact that I came out of the Jeep accident with only a smashed-up ankle. She was"—Fletcher stopped speaking and cleared his throat roughly—"Nance, that little girl was killed a week after I took her picture. There was an enemy raid on her village, and she . . . was shot."

"Oh, my God," Nancy whispered.

"I'd given her a peppermint stick. It was wrapped in cellophane, and she used to run her finger over it, back and forth, so that the paper would make noise. I tried to show her how to take the cellophane off so that she could eat the candy. She just clutched it in her little hands and shook her head. She wanted to save it, I guess. When we went into the village after the raid, I found her. She—she was holding the peppermint stick. They buried her like that, with her precious candy in her tiny hand. I'll never . . . forget her."

Tears spilled onto Nancy's cheeks as she rushed into Fletcher's embrace and felt his strong arms enfold her. He buried his face in the fragrant cloud of her curls as she rested her head on his chest, fighting back her tears, and knowing from the way he was breathing that Fletcher was striving to control his own emotions.

What an incredible man she loved, Nancy thought. What a warm, giving, caring human being. The work of David Forester reflected the image of a man with a soul of great depths, with a great capacity for loving. And he loved *her*. David Forester, Fletcher McGill, intertwined, one and the same, loved her. And she loved him.

She lifted her head, causing him to lift his, and their eyes met.

"I love you, Fletcher," she said softly. "I love you with my whole heart, with all that I am. I truly love you."

She felt him stiffen, but before she could question why, before she could wonder what would cause his unexpected reaction to her declaration of love, his mouth came down hard on hers, erasing all thought from her mind. His heat invaded her body, igniting her passion and bringing a purr of pleasure from her throat.

She loved him, Fletcher thought wildly. Nance loved him. She'd said the words he'd longed to hear, ached to hear. But, dammit, who had she said them to? Fletcher McGill of Fletcher's Pond? or Fletcher McGill/David Forester? No, he wouldn't torture himself like that, question the timing of Nancy's declaration of love. But if only she'd said it before, if only she'd—No, it didn't matter. He wouldn't allow it to matter.

"Nance," he muttered as he lifted his head, "let's get out of here."

"Yes," she said breathlessly. "But what about your photographs, everything that's happening out there?"

"Selene will handle it. I'm just another patron of

the gallery, as far as anyone is concerned. No one knows who I am."

"Imagine the excitement it would cause if they knew that David Forester was among them," she said, smiling up at him.

"David Forester doesn't really exist, Nancy," he said, frowning.

"Of course he does. He's a part of you, a wonderful part. I'm so glad you told me all of this, Fletcher. I'm so very proud of you, of what you've done."

"Of what David Forester has done, you mean," he said, moving her away from him. "How do you feel about plain old Fletcher McGill?"

"Fletcher, what is it? What's wrong? Your eyes have turned ice-cold. If I've said something to upset you, I wish you'd tell me what it is."

"No," he said, shaking his head, "it's not anything you've said. I'm just tired. This has been a killer to pull off in such a short length of time."

"And you did it for me. To give me back those six years."

"Yes."

"Thank you, Fletcher. I thank you, and I love you."

He looked at her for a long moment, then jerked his head toward the door. "Let's go."

Nancy collected her shawl and purse from the chair, telling herself that there was nothing wrong. Fletcher was tired, that was all. He'd put in a grueling few days, plus the emotionally draining evening they'd just spent. He wasn't acting strangely; he was simply exhausted.

"All set," she said, and walked out the door. She was tired, too, she realized. She was emotionally drained from attempting to comprehend all that Fletcher had told her.

Her gaze flickered over the large photographs on the walls as they made their way to the front door. David Forester, she mused. Fletcher was David Forester. It was still hard to believe. He had given so much to so many people during the six years he'd been gone. And now he was home. He was home, he loved her, and she loved him. The future, at last, was theirs to have, together. They'd talk, make plans, and . . . But the first thing on the agenda was for Mr. McGill to get some sleep. She had thought, perhaps, that tonight he would take her into his arms and . . . No, he was totally exhausted.

"Oh, Fletcher, look at the stars," she said when they stepped outside.

He handed the valet his parking stub. "They were there when we came in."

"They were? I didn't see them."

"You were a bit up-tight. I guess maybe this was all rather dramatic, but I thought it was the best way to do it. There's the car. Geez, that kid drives like a lunatic."

Nancy sank into the plush seat with a contented sigh and smiled over at Fletcher as he pulled out of the parking lot.

"Are you hungry?" she asked. "We didn't eat very much dinner."

"No. Are you?"

"No. Is your ankle bothering you?"

"No."

"Do your parents know that you're David Forester?"

"Not yet. I'll tell them now that I've told you. It has to be kept quiet, though, Nance, because of the terms of my book contract. We'll have to give some thought as to whether or not to tell Kip now. I'm not saying he can't be trusted, but he's young, and if he got excited, he could let something slip. I'll think about it."

"I'm very honored that you told me even before telling your parents."

"That's the way I wanted to do it, in the proper order," he said. It was her declaration of love that was out of order. Oh, McGill, knock it off. He was tired, and needed about twenty hours of sleep. He was putting too much emphasis on the wrong thing because he was exhausted and his brain was fuzzy. Enough was enough. Nancy loved him, pure and simple. But if only . . . No!

Nancy loved him. He had spanned the gap of the missing six years, brought the past up to the present, brought the memories of what they had shared at Fletcher's Pond during that long-ago summer into the here and now.

Fletcher's Pond, where he had first made love to his Nance.

And tonight? he asked himself as he maneuvered through the traffic. He loved her, she loved him, and. . .

"I want you, Nance," he said, his voice low and husky. "I want to make love to you." Lord above, McGill, he fumed, what a helluva thing to say while driving along a busy street. He was as romantic as a turnip.

Thank goodness, Nancy thought. She'd been afraid he was too tired. She'd waited six years for this. Tonight was theirs. "And I want you, Fletcher. As they say in the movies, 'Your place, or mine?' "

He glanced over at her, shock evident on his face.

And then he smiled. It was a warm smile, a joyous smile, a smile that reminded Nancy of the younger Fletcher she'd known so long ago. She matched his expression, then laughed softly when he ran a red light.

Fletcher McGill, she mused, was David Forester, world-famous photographer. But not tonight. Tonight they were just Fletcher and Nancy, of Oakville, Georgia. Fletcher and Nance, of Fletcher's Pond.

Eight

When Nancy and Fletcher stepped into the living room of her hotel suite, he turned immediately, startling her as he reached above her to close the door with the palm of his hand. His abrupt movement caused her to lean back against the door as Fletcher towered above her.

Their eyes met, and Nancy's heart began to race as she saw the raw desire reflected in Fletcher's eyes. His body wasn't touching hers, but she could feel the heat of him, feel the coiled tension of want and need that was weaving from him through her. She'd left one small lamp on, and the sexuality in the softly glowing room seemed to sweep over them in waves, as Nancy felt a pulsing warmth deep, deep within her.

Fletcher slid his hand down the door to the side of her head, then moved closer, still not touching her as he braced his other hand on the door, trapping her in a cage of sensual power.

"I'm closing that door on the world," he said, his voice gritty. "No one exists but the two of us. Just us, Nance. The way it was at Fletcher's Pond."

"Yes," was all she could manage to say as a wondrous trembling coursed through her. She filled her senses with all of Fletcher and with the heat that continued to weave into her, stirring her desire, kindling it into a roaring flame.

"I love you, Nancy."

His voice flowed over her, and she ached with the sweet pain of anticipation, of a want so intense, it was like none before. She closed her eyes for a fleeting moment, then looked at him again; at his smoldering eyes, the rugged planes of his handsome, tanned face, then shifted her gaze to his lips, willing them to claim hers. Her body tingled and trembled and burned.

Dear Lord, how she wanted him.

"And I love you, Fletcher," she said, hearing the breathless quality in her voice.

He dipped his head and brushed his lips over hers, returning to skim his tongue along the same path. Nancy shivered. He nipped at the corners of her mouth, then sucked, just for a moment, on her bottom lip. She lifted her hands to grip his arms for support, her purse and shawl falling unnoticed to the floor.

Fletcher's hands inched closer; then his fingers wove through her curls, holding her head steady as his lips came close, so close, to hers.

"Tell me again that you love me," he said, his

voice raspy. "Say, 'I love you, Fletcher McGill. Just you, Fletcher McGill.' Say it, Nance."

"I love you, Fletcher McGill," she whispered. "I have never stopped loving you. I will love you until the day I die."

With a groan Fletcher dropped his hands to splay on her back as his mouth melted over hers. He drew her up against him, molding her to him as she lifted her arms to circle his neck. Their tongues met, tasting, savoring, sparking passions ever higher.

Fletcher found the zipper at the back of Nancy's dress and pulled it down, his fingers sliding along her soft skin. He lifted his head and brushed the material away to fall in a peach-colored pool at her feet. Her breasts were bare, and he sucked in his breath as his gaze traveled over them.

"Beautiful," he murmured. "Even more beautiful than I remember." He filled his palms with the feminine bounty. "Ah, Nancy, I've dreamed of this, ached for this, for so damn long."

He lowered his head and drew one nipple into his mouth, hearing Nancy's soft sigh of pleasure. The bud grew taut, responded to the rhythmic pull of his mouth, and his manhood surged. He moved to the other breast, suckling, teasing, tasting . . .

Remembering.

She was all, and she was more, than he'd lived with in his heart, mind, and soul for the past six years, Fletcher thought hazily. She was child, she was woman. She was innocence, in that she knew only him, only him. She was his. His Nance. He was home.

He moved reluctantly from her breasts, drawing his thumbs over the tight, moist nipples. He went lower, trailing light kisses across her stomach, feeling her tremble from the feathery journey. He hooked his thumbs in the band of her panty hose and inched them down, catching the wispy material of her bikini panties as he went. Lower. His breathing was rough, his heart thudded in his chest, and his blood pounded in his veins. Lower.

"Fletcher," she gasped.

"Beautiful. And mine."

She gripped his shoulders as he slid her shoes off, first one, then the other. She stepped free of the pool of clothing. Fletcher straightened, his gaze sweeping over her, seeming to heat a path wherever his eyes traveled. She was naked before him, offering him all that she was, and she felt . . . beautiful.

And wanted.

And she remembered.

She remembered the girl and the boy, but now knew this was the woman and the man. She had no more experience than on the night he had left her, but she had changed, grown, now rejoiced in her own femininity rather than being in childish awe. The novice had been taught, and the teacher stood before her. Hers.

Fletcher lifted her into his arms and carried her into the bedroom beyond. The drapes stood open, flooding the area with a silvery luminescence that cast a spell of magic over the night. He set her on her feet, swept back the blankets, then placed her on the cool sheets.

"I could never capture you on film," he said, his voice thick. He stood by the bed, his gaze once more roving over her lissome form. "A camera couldn't see the goodness, the gentleness, within you. A camera couldn't know how you trust me, give yourself to me so totally, holding nothing back. Only I know, because you are mine."

"Oh, Fletcher, please," she said, nearly sobbing, "come to me. I want to see you, all of you. Touch you, all of you. Feel you, all of you, inside me."

He shed his clothes, and Nancy watched. As each part of his tanned, muscled body came into her view, her desire grew. His manhood surged with the want and need of her, only her, and a liquid heat burned deep inside her.

Naked before her, Fletcher hesitated, curling his hands into tight fists as he strove for control before daring to move onto the bed, before daring to touch her again.

"Fletcher."

She said his name in a seductive whisper and lifted her arm to receive him into her embrace. He groaned and went to her, stretching out next to her, carefully shifting the cast away from her soft skin. He splayed one hand on her stomach as he rested on his other elbow, gazing down at her with a message of need in his dark eyes that was matched by the hard evidence of his arousal pressing against her.

"I want to go slowly and make it perfect for you," he said huskily. "But, Nance, I'm about to explode. I don't think you have any idea how beautiful you look lying there."

She smiled, a lovely, womanly, serene smile, then dropped her gaze to inch over him—slowly, so slowly—savoring all that she saw. All that he was. All that would be hers. Again. At last. She lifted her hand

and trailed her fingers through the moist, tawny curls on his chest, feeling his shudder of response.

There was such sensual pleasure in touching him, she mused dreamily. He was magnificent, her Fletcher. So bronzed and tightly muscled, so hard where she was soft. Her counterpart, the man to her woman, the other half of her being.

"Come to me, Fletcher," she whispered. "We have all night. I need you so much. You don't have to go slowly. I don't want you to. I've waited too long. Waited for you."

His mouth swept down over hers in a searing kiss, his tongue delving deep inside her mouth, and moving in a rhythm that matched the pulsing heat low and deep inside her. His hand slid over her to the apex of her thighs, his fingers gently seeking the very essence of her.

"Oh, Nance," he said, lifting his head a fraction of an inch, "you do want me. You're so ready for me."

"Yes. Oh, yes."

He moved over her, catching his weight on his forearms as he shifted the cast between her legs. Nancy slid her arms around his strong back, urging him closer.

But Fletcher savored the moment, his muscles quivering from forced restraint as he looked at her face, saw the desire in the smoky blue hue of her eyes, her kiss-swollen lips, which were moist and slightly parted, inviting his tongue to enter yet again.

He nipped lightly at her lips, then shifted lower to draw the bud of one breast deep, so deep, into his mouth. Nancy burrowed her fingers into his thick hair and pressed his mouth harder onto her throbbing breast, a moan escaping from her lips.

"Please," she whispered. "I need you, I want you."

"Soon," he said. He moved to the other breast and laved it with his tongue, his heart thudding against his ribs. He lifted his head to look directly into her eyes. "Nance, it's been so long for you. I don't want to hurt you. I couldn't handle it if I hurt you."

"You won't. Oh, please don't make me wait any longer. Please." She arched her back to raise her hips to his, feeling his manhood surge more strongly against her. "Please."

Fletcher groaned, then entered her.

Slowly.

He gritted his teeth to gather every ounce of control he possessed as he moved into her, watching her face for any sign of pain, waiting for her body to accommodate him, then going farther into her honeyed warmth.

Slowly.

Nancy thought she would die from the need of him.

Slowly, he filled her with all that he was, then held still, his body glistening with perspiration.

"Oh . . . yes," she said, her eyes half closed. "Yes."

She lifted her hips, and Fletcher lost control.

He began a thundering cadence, a raging rhythm like a tempestuous storm giving way to its power. Nancy matched his tempo, giving, taking, reaching.

"Say my name," Fletcher gasped out. "Tell me who's making love with you. Say it!"

"Fletcher. My Fletcher McGill. My Fletcher . . . Oh, dear heaven. . . Oh, Fletcher, hold me."

"I'm here. I'm right here."

He felt the spasms ripple through her, felt her body tighten around him in invitation to join him in the place of splendor where she had gone. He watched her face, saw the epitome of femininity she was experiencing create a beauty beyond description. Wave after wave swept through her, and at last he joined her, thrusting hard and deep within her, his body going taut, then pulsing, passing all he was from him into her. Ecstasy.

And neither remembered the past, for this was new, inexplicably different from anything they had experienced together before. It was a meshing not only of bodies, but of hearts, minds, and souls. They were joined beyond the physical, interwoven into one entity that encompassed every facet of their beings.

They lingered in the wondrous place, drifted, sighed in contentment, then came slowly and gently back to the now. Fletcher brushed his lips over Nancy's, then shifted off her, pulling her close as he covered them with the blankets.

Neither spoke.

Each searched for the words to describe their glorious union, their celebration of being one, but found no way to express verbally all that it had been. And so neither spoke.

It was a lovely silence, a peaceful, sated silence, as they lay nestled in each other's arms. Minutes passed. The room was still, cloaked in the silvery glow of the moon and stars. The night held its magic. They slept. Without having said one word.

Nancy stirred, then reached out her hand to seek Fletcher's warmth. The empty expanse of bed next to her caused her to open her eyes in alarm. She glanced quickly at the clock, saw that it was just after three in the morning. Then her gaze swept over the room.

Fletcher was standing in front of the window, one fist braced high on the frame. The moonlight poured over him like a silvery waterfall, and Nancy felt her pulse skitter as she drank in the sight of his powerful nude body. Memories of their lovemaking crept in around her, and she felt the familiar thrum of desire deep within her.

How glorious it had been, she mused. Such beauty, such completeness. She and Fletcher had gone beyond what they had known together at Fletcher's Pond. Perhaps it was because they were older, more mature, more capable of understanding the true depths of love itself. She didn't know, and it didn't really matter how the past compared to the present. What was important was now, and the tomorrows to follow. Dear heaven, how she loved that man.

But then she frowned. Why was Fletcher standing by the window? she wondered. He'd been so tired, she'd have thought he'd sleep until noon. What had called him from her side to stand alone?

As she watched him stare out over the sleeping city, she suddenly recalled his demanding she say his name as they made love. She'd forgotten about it in the lovely, drowsy aftermath, but now she could clearly hear the frantic edge to his voice. He had needed, desperately needed, to have her say that it was he, Fletcher McGill, with whom she was sharing such ecstasy.

Nancy continued to stare at Fletcher's rigid body, her mind whirling. She sifted and sorted through past conversations, heard again and again Fletcher's emphasis on how important it was to him to be accepted for himself, for the man he was. It went back to his youth, she realized, to Oakville and the line of distinction between the powerful and the lowly in the small town. And king of the hill, mightier than the mighty, were the McGills. There, too, at home, he'd fought for acceptance, hoping, wishing, his father would see that Fletcher wasn't another Shane.

And Fletcher had hated every minute of it.

The pattern of his life was set early on by his driving need to break free of labels, to rebel, to be recognized as an individual, not one of an elite group. Whether he was excelling in sports or getting into trouble with endless pranks, he didn't care, as long as he was known as himself.

And now? she mused. Now there was David Forester. Fletcher had broken free of the McGill name and reputation, only to create another nemesis for himself in the form of David Forester. He would once again be struggling against the haunting ghosts of his boyhood; wondering, watching, waiting to see if people sought him out because they sincerely liked Fletcher McGill or because he was the famous David Forester.

Well, this time, Nancy thought decisively, things were different. Fletcher wasn't alone with his doubts and fears. She was there by his side, and she loved him. She understood him so much better now. She'd listened, really listened, when he'd spoken. He would come to see that everything they faced would be easier to deal with because there were two of them against the foe.

Her breath caught in her throat as Fletcher's shoulders suddenly slumped and he bent his head. He looked so alone and lonely, and without thinking she slid off the bed and went to him, wrapping her arms around his waist and resting her head on his back.

"I didn't mean to wake you," he said, covering her hands with his.

"You didn't." She paused. "Do you want to talk about what's bothering you?"

Right, Fletcher thought dryly. Just whip it on her, let her find out that he was insane. Tell her he'd wakened in a cold sweat, his heart thudding painfully in his chest. Tell her how he'd had a nightmare in which he saw her standing in front of a throng of people, announcing that she was in love with David Forester. "What about Fletcher McGill?" someone had asked, and Nancy had said, "Who?" then waved breezily, saying David was waiting for her. David Forester, the man she loved. Tell her all that? She'd probably head for the door, after informing him he should have himself shipped to the farm.

"Fletcher?"

He turned in her arms, pulling her close and forcing a smile. "I'm okay. I just have a lot on my mind, that's all."

"Like what?"

Demons. Fears. Shadowy ghosts from childhood. Foes that could very well be stronger than he was. "Lots of things. Us, for example. Our future plans together."

"Oh. Well, we have plenty of time to talk about that. Don't you think you should get some sleep?"

He slid his hands down over her naked buttocks

and cradled her against him, the action having an immediate effect on his body.

"Sleep?" he repeated.

She moved her hands up his chest. "Or . . . whatever."

He chuckled. "Such as? A game of gin rummy? A debate on the state of the economy?" She wiggled seductively against him. He cleared his throat roughly. "Guess not. Just what is it you had in mind, Miss Forest?"

She walked her fingers back down his chest, then lower, and lower yet.

"Oh, Nance," Fletcher said, with a groan and a laugh. "In about two seconds this discussion will be closed and the decision made."

"Oh-h-h?" she said, batting her eyelashes at him.

He swept her up into his arms. "Yep."

"What are we going to do?"

"Checkers. I'm crazy about checkers," he said, striding toward the bed. He laid her on the rumpled sheets. "I'm going to get dressed, go find someplace that's open all night, and buy a set of checkers. Do you want to be red or black? I'm telling you, Nance, I'm really into checkers. I remember the time—"

"Fletcher McGill," she said, laughing, "you have two seconds to get into this bed and do wonderful things to my body."

"Sold."

It was one smooth, powerful motion. Fletcher moved over her and into her. Nancy received all that he was with a soft sigh of pleasure, then wrapped her legs around his thighs, lifting her hips, bringing him closer. There was nothing tentative, nothing slow about Fletcher's lovemaking this time. The rhythm began in strong, steady strokes; deeper, harder, carrying her up and away and over the edge of reality.

"Fletcher!"

"Yes." He groaned, then shuddered above her as they reached the ultimate goal only seconds apart. He collapsed against her, then moments later pushed himself up to rest on his forearms. He kissed her, a hard, mind-drugging kiss, then moved away with a satisfied-sounding sigh. "Know what?" he asked yawning.

"What?"

"That was better than checkers."

Nancy laughed, then curled up next to him spoon fashion, her back to his front. He slid his arm beneath her breasts and dropped a light kiss on her shoulder. He inhaled her aroma, which was feminine and uniquely hers, combined with the musky, sensual scent of their lovemaking.

She was asleep already, Fletcher realized, hearing her soft, steady breathing. She was like a contented kitten, cozy and warm. Lord, how he loved her. At moments like this, it seemed impossible that there could be room in his world for doubts and fears. But they came, they always came; haunting him, taunting him, chilling him to the very recesses of his soul.

How could it be, he thought fiercely, that a man who had seen what he had, gone where he'd gone, wasn't stronger within himself? He had trekked through uncharted jungles, hiked up mountains not really knowing what was at the top, taken rickety boats down angry rivers. He'd slept on the ground with a gun by his hand, eaten food that had questionable origin, gone on alone when a guide had refused to go farther. He'd sought and found the faces, the special ones, the faces of life the world over.

He'd known fear in his journey, and had been close to death on more than one occasion. But he'd always won. With brute strength, cunning, or plain old luck, he'd come out on top. He was a doer, a fighter, a man who faced a challenge head on and settled for no less than the best he could do.

Nancy sighed in her sleep, and Fletcher tightened his hold on her, fitting her more snugly to him, and feeling the heated stirrings in the lower regions of his body.

She had declared her love for him, said the words he'd ached to hear again after so many years. She'd given herself to him in total abandon and trust, and placed herself in his safekeeping as she gave way to her passion. There was no reason, no damn reason, to doubt that she really loved *him*, Fletcher McGill, just as she had at Fletcher's Pond.

But he was also David Forester.

And Nancy had declared her love out of order, after the fact, after knowing that David Forester existed.

She hadn't lied about her love for him, Fletcher decided firmly. She truly believed what she had said. But she could have lost touch with herself, forgotten how adamantly she had stated that the past was over, she was going on with her life alone, and that his feelings for her didn't matter.

Then David Forester had emerged.

And Nancy had said how much she loved him.

Out of order.

His inner demons had the power to destroy him.

If Nancy's love was genuine, Fletcher knew, his doubts and fears could crush it into dust, and along with it, him.

Fletcher sighed, a weary sigh, tired of body and of mind. He had to find the answers. And soon, he knew, because he couldn't go on like this. The rest of his life was at stake—his future, his Nance, everything.

At last he slept, but it wasn't a peaceful slumber. It was plagued by disturbing dreams, twisting and turning pictures that brought a moan from his lips. He saw Nancy, then his father, laughing at him, shaking their heads, then walking away arm in arm. And he saw the little girl, the "Child of the Silent Eyes," clutching her peppermint stick as a single tear slid down her cheek. He saw himself standing in a fog, lost and alone.

When Nancy awoke the next morning at nine, Fletcher was still asleep. He was sprawled on his stomach, the sheet to his waist, his tanned, muscled back bare and beckoning her to run her hands over the taut skin. She gazed at him, a soft smile on her lips, marveling at his magnificent beauty, reliving in her mind once more the ecstasy of their lovemaking.

Today, maybe, she mused, stretching leisurely, they would talk about their future plans. She had a job waiting for her here in Atlanta, at Cory Computer. Fletcher had a book to write. A person could write a book anywhere, couldn't he? Or could he? She didn't know anything about writing a book. Well, they'd work it all out.

Mrs. Fletcher McGill, she thought, practicing. Nancy McGill. Nancy Forest McGill. Heavenly. Well, she supposed at times she'd be called Mrs. David Forester. To the world at large, that was who Fletcher would be once his book was published. Whatever, it made no difference. To her, he was Fletcher, her Fletcher, who had loved her at Fletcher's Pond, and who loved her now. That was all that mattered. Those who sought him out because he was David Forester wouldn't get beyond the door that she and Fletcher closed on the outside world. A strong door, because it was created by both of them. Fletcher would come to realize that, know he wasn't alone, know that together they could beat the demons of his youth and set him free of old ghosts forever.

The future, their future, was going to be glorious!

Smiling brightly, Nancy eased off the bed, collected clean clothes, and went into the bathroom. Certain, intimate parts of her body were sore, and she savored the knowledge that it was because of Fletcher's delectable lovemaking. After a soothing shower she dressed in navy blue twill slacks, a blue-and-white flowered blouse, and arranged her curls with a few flicks of the hairbrush. When she stepped out of the bathroom, she saw that Fletcher was still sleeping.

Good, she decided, going into the living room. He'd been exhausted, and needed the rest.

Good grief, she thought an instant later. There were her clothes in a heap by the door. It wouldn't take a genius to figure out what had taken place there.

She scooped up the things, folded them, then placed them on a chair. What she'd really like, she mused, was a cup of coffee. Should she wait for Fletcher to wake up? Call for room service? Go to the coffee shop?

The coffee shop won the vote, and she propped a note on the nightstand for Fletcher, then left the suite. Downstairs she bought a newspaper, settled into a booth in the café, and ordered coffee and a sweet roll. She opened the paper to the section titled "Atlanta's Arts," and within moments was smiling.

"You're chipper this morning," the waitress said, placing the coffee and roll on the table.

"What? Oh, I was just reading the review of David Forester's exhibition last night. This critic was highly complimentary."

"I heard about that fancy deal," the waitress said. "I served breakfast to some folks who'd flown in from Mobile for it. They said it was wonderful. I've seen that David Forester's work in magazines. Some of those faces are marvelous, but others? They give me goose bumps. It's like the people are real, and are looking right into my mind. I can't believe what that man can do with a camera."

Among other things, Nancy thought smugly. "He's very good," she said. Oh, that was putting it mildly. Mercy, shame on her.

The waitress leaned over. "I know who David Forester really is," she whispered. "Those folks from Mobile told me."

"Oh?" Nancy said, frowning slightly.

"You won't tell anyone if I tell you?"

"No."

"Well, okay." The woman glanced around first. "David Forester is really Henry Kissinger."

Nancy nearly choked on the laughter she forced herself to swallow. "Really?" she asked, widening her eyes. "No kidding? You're sure?"

"Yep," the waitress said, appearing extremely pleased with herself.

"Well, I'm just truly amazed, truly."

"So was I. Now, don't tell a soul, you hear?"

"Don't worry about a thing," Nancy said.

"I gotta go check on my customers. I'll be back to refill your coffee cup."

"Thank you," Nancy said. Henry Kissinger? Wait until Fletcher heard this. He'd fall apart laughing. Little did anyone know that David Forester was upstairs at that very moment, naked as a jaybird, and dead to the world in bed. Henry Kissinger? Fletcher was really going to get a kick out of this.

Nancy glanced through the remainder of the paper while she ate her light breakfast. When she came to the want ads, she realized how recently it had been that she'd bought an Atlanta paper to look for an apartment. An apartment she'd planned to live in alone. Now everything had changed. She wasn't alone, not any longer. She was half of a whole, one of a two, part of a couple, and a whole bunch of other lovely ways to say that she loved Fletcher and he loved her. They were together. Again. Only this time, it was forever.

She ordered a large coffee to be placed in a Styrofoam cup with a lid to take to Fletcher, tucked the newspaper under her arm, paid her bill, and went back upstairs to the suite.

Fletcher was still sleeping.

Nancy smiled, shook her head, then placed the newspaper, opened to the review, on the nightstand with the coffee. She curled up in the corner of the sofa in the living room to read a magazine that had been provided, compliments of the hotel.

A short tme later, the rustling of paper caused her to look up. Fletcher was standing naked in the bedroom doorway, the newspaper clutched tightly in his hand. His hair was tousled from sleep, and there was a stormy expression on his face.

Nancy smiled at him. "Good morning. Why do I get the feeling you don't wake up like Mr. Sunshine?"

"What in the hell is this?" He strode forward and tossed the newspaper onto the sofa.

"The morning paper," she said, frowning in confusion.

"You sure didn't waste any time, did you?" he said tersely, planting his hands on his narrow hips. "You just hightailed it downstairs at the crack of dawn to see what was being said about the great David Forester. Well, guess what? Fletcher McGill didn't appreciate waking up in an empty bed."

"Oh, now, wait just a minute here," Nancy said, scrambling to her feet. "In the first place, I did not leave at the crack of dawn. Secondly, I went for a cup of coffee, as evidenced by the one I brought you. And thirdly, if there is such a word, I thought you might be pleased to know that you received an excellent review."

"I don't give a hoot in hell about my reviews!" he yelled.

"Well, excuse me for breathing," she said, matching his volume.

"Did you get a high, reading that syrupy crap?" Fletcher raved on, pointing to the paper. "Did you say to yourself that you'd been to bed with the famous David Forester?"

Nancy narrowed her eyes. "Rumor has it," she said tightly, "that I've been to bed with Henry Kissinger."

"What?"

"Oh, forget it," she said, throwing up her hands. "This is ridiculous. You don't like reviews? Fine. You could have just said so without screaming at me."

"You're missing the point," he said, raking a hand through his hair.

"Oh? Then why don't you explain to me just what the point is? I love you, Fletcher, but that doesn't make me automatically capable of reading your mind."

Praise the Lord for that much, Fletcher thought. If she could read his mind, she'd head for the hills. There he stood, sounding like a jealous lover. Sounding like a Loony Tune because he was jealous of himself! He was losing it. Totally losing it.

"I'm sorry," he said quietly. "It jarred me to find you weren't in bed when I woke up. Then the first thing I saw was this junk about David Forester, and I didn't feel like dealing with him right now. I really am sorry, Nance. Thank you for the coffee."

She smiled, then crossed the room and circled his waist with her arms. "You're forgiven, crabby. By the way, I love your outfit. Bare body and a cast. It's very voguish."

Fletcher enfolded her in his arms, pulling her tightly to him. He buried his face in her fragrant curls for a moment, then drew a steadying, deep breath as he lifted his head. Nancy felt a shudder ripple through him.

"Fletcher," she said, looking up at him and searching his face for an answer, "are you all right?"

"Sure," he said, forcing a smile. "Come sit on the

bed with me while I drink my coffee. I promise to be more human after my caffeine fix."

"You feel very human right now," she said, sliding her hands over his taut buttocks.

"Could I have my coffee before you jump my bones?" he asked, grinning at her.

She sighed dramatically. "I guess so, if you really insist."

"Come on." He circled her shoulders with his arm and started toward the bedroom. "And you have three seconds to explain the Henry Kissinger remark."

Nancy laughed, but sobered again as she glanced back at the crumpled newspaper lying on the sofa.

Nine

At midnight that night Nancy gave up the attempt to sleep and left her bed to sit in the rocking chair by the window. There were no twinkling stars or shining moon that night to cast a silvery, magic glow over Oakville. The clouds were thick, the air heavy with the feel and smell of pending rain. Thunder rumbled in the distance.

Nancy sighed, aware that she was at odds with herself. She'd been carrying on an inner dialogue since going to bed two hours before. She had told herself over and over that the weekend in Atlanta with Fletcher had been wonderful, beautiful, fantastic. But in the next breath she would admit that during the entire day there had been something wrong, an underlying current of tension emanating from Fletcher.

On the surface he'd appeared relaxed and carefree. They'd had a leisurely lunch, then strolled through a group of small, unique shops until Fletcher's ankle had tired. They'd found a quiet park and sat on the grass, watching the families of ducks cavorting in a pond. They'd spoken of unimportant things. Fletcher had not brought up the topic of the future, their plans, Nancy's job in Atlanta, or when he needed to begin work on his book.

There was nothing wrong with that, Nancy had reasoned after pushing aside her initial disappointment. Fletcher was obviously taking the day off from heavy thinking, which everyone had the right to do.

But it had been there, the tension within him, the unspoken whatever it was that had seemed to make him grow more distant as the hours of the day passed.

After dinner they had driven back to Oakville, with Fletcher following Nancy along the highway. At the edge of Oakville he'd honked and waved, then gone in the opposite direction toward the McGill estate. Nancy had driven the remaining few blocks to her little house, filled with a strange chill of gloom and doom.

She had been grateful that there was a major-league baseball game on TV to hold Kip's attention when she arrived home. Yes, she'd told him, she'd had a lovely time. No, she and Fletcher hadn't made plans to get married, they'd simply enjoyed some pleasant hours away from the nosy noses of Oakville. Kip had shrugged, said it all sounded very boring, but that his orgy had been a huge success. Nancy had whopped him with a throw pillow.

But now, in the darkness, with the storm clouds racing across the Georgia sky, Nancy could not escape from the fact that something was bothering

Fletcher. And, she was sure it had to do with David Forester. What she couldn't grasp was why Fletcher seemed to be withdrawing from *her.* She loved him; he knew that. She loved Fletcher McGill of Fletcher's Pond; he knew that. She'd never stopped loving him in the six long years he'd been gone, and he knew that.

Then why, why, was he acting so strangely, seeming to watch her, to measure her words, until she'd been ready to scream in nervous frustration? How could it be that after the lovemaking they'd shared, the complete giving, the becoming one, that she'd looked up so many times during the day to see him staring at her as though she were a stranger? Darn it, what was wrong with Fletcher McGill?

He'd changed his mind, she thought suddenly, sitting bolt upright. He didn't love her. He didn't want to marry her. He didn't want to have a future with her after all. He wanted . . . he wanted to jog around the world taking pictures, and hopping into bed with sophisticated women who didn't look like peach yogurt. She'd kill him!

"Oh, Nancy, shut up," she said, slouching back in the rocker. Fletcher loved her. She knew he did.

All she could do was wait.

And she would.

Because she loved him.

Nancy sighed, got to her feet, and went back to bed. A heavy rain started, pounding on the roof like a thousand drummers beating a cadence. She blanked her mind, listened to the rain, and finally slept.

Fletcher stared at the amber liquid in his glass,

swirled it around, then downed it in a single swallow, cringing as it burned his throat. He glanced up at the ceiling of the living room as he heard the rain begin to fall, then redirected his attention to the bottle on the small bar. He splashed more liquor into his glass.

"You look," his father said from the doorway, "like a man who is determined to get as drunk as a skunk."

"Got it in one," Fletcher said sullenly. "Care to join me?'"

"You can pour me a shot," Dennis said, coming over to the bar. "I would suggest, though, that you sit down, before you fall down. I'd think that a broken ankle is enough for now."

"Good point." Fletcher grabbed the bottle, weaved his way rather unsteadily to the sofa, and sat down heavily.

Dennis poured himself a small drink and sat opposite Fletcher in a leather chair. Fletcher tossed off his drink, then refilled his glass.

"You're going to feel like hell in the morning, son," Dennis said.

"Yep."

"I'm not quite sure why you're doing this. If I thought you were celebrating, I'd understand. What you told your mother and me tonight about your being David Forester is certainly cause to be proud, and I lift my glass to you. You are not, however, in a festive mood."

"Nope."

"So, it has to be woman trouble. Doesn't she love you anymore, Fletcher?"

"She loves me," he said, then took a hefty swallow of liquor. "Yep, she does."

"And you love her."

"Yep," Fletcher said.

"But there's a problem," his father said.

"Yep," Fletcher said, and drained his glass.

"Care to share it?"

Fletcher blinked once, very slowly. "It has to do, sir"—he hiccupped—"with the correct order of things."

Dennis frowned. "I see." He paused. "No, I don't. I have no idea what you're talking about. Correct order of what things?"

"Love," Fletcher said much too loudly, pointing a finger in the air. "She's out of order." He filled his glass.

"Love. Out of order," Dennis repeated. "Are you saying she's pregnant, which is out of order because you haven't married her yet? I'd have said you haven't been back long enough to know if she's pregnant."

"Pregnant?" Fletcher repeated, his eyes widening. "Oh-h-h." He smiled crookedly. "A little baby. Wouldn't that be nice? A baby girl that looks like my Nance." He frowned. "No, she isn't pregnant. Not that I know of, anyway."

"So much for that. Well, I'm still confused. At least now I know she has a name."

"Of course she has a name, sir," Fletcher said, blinking several times. "She's Nance. She's Nancy Forest. My Nance. And I'm Fletcher of Fletcher's Pond. However"—he hiccupped again—"Fletcher's Pond is a secret."

"Oh," Dennis said, smiling into his glass. "Then don't tell me about Fletcher's Pond."

"I won't."

"Tell me about love's being out of order."

"Not love, per se, but the declaration of that love," Fletcher said, his words slurring together. "The timing shrinks . . . I mean, stinks. He was already there."

"He who?"

"David Forester."

"Oh, I see," Dennis said slowly. "Yes, I think I do. Your Nancy told **you** she still loved you after you revealed that you **were** David Forester."

"Yep."

"Ah-h-h." Dennis nodded. "I get the picture. And that's how it's been all your life, hasn't it? Your wanting to be accepted as a person, an individual, not as a McGill, and now not as David Forester, but just as Fletcher."

"Yep," Fletcher said, then tilted slightly to the left.

"Fletcher, before you pass out, listen to me."

"You bet," Fletcher said, smiling pleasantly. "I'm all years . . . ears."

"You're not giving yourself enough credit. You are one of the finest men I know. If you love this Nancy Forest, then she has to be a very fine woman, so you're not giving her enough credit, either. Forget the past, Fletcher. Look to the future. That's where your happiness lies."

"But . . . it's wrong. . . . She said it . . . out of order."

Dennis got quickly to his feet and took the glass and bottle from Fletcher's hands. Fletcher toppled sideways onto the sofa cushions with a groan, and in the next minute began to snore. Dennis tugged and pushed until he straightened the heavy, inert body along the sofa, then covered him with an afghan. He frowned as he looked down at Fletcher.

"Forgive me, son," he said quietly. "This is my doing, from the time you were a boy. I'm sorry, Fletcher. Dear Lord, I am so sorry." With dragging steps, Dennis turned and left the room.

When Nancy arrived home from work the next day, she saw Hank Bloom, her real-estate agent, standing on her front porch.

Hank Bloom, she thought dismally as she pulled into the driveway, was not Fletcher McGill. She'd waited all day to hear from Fletcher, had jumped every time the telephone had rung at the dentist's office, and craned her neck to see who was coming in when she'd heard the door open.

But no Fletcher.

Driving home, she'd created a scenario in which Fletcher would be sitting on the front steps when she arrived, would sweep her into his arms, kiss her senseless, and tell her forty-two times in a row that he loved her. And tell her that there was absolutely, positively nothing wrong.

So who did she get? she thought dryly. Pudgy little Hank Bloom, who looked like a close descendant of a Smurf. Great.

"Hello, Fancy Nancy," Hank said as she got out of the car.

Nancy gritted her teeth. He'd called her that since they'd been in the third grade. Stupid. "Hi," she said, forcing a smile.

He waved some papers in the air. "I got an offer on your house. Remember that young couple with the baby? He just got on at the mill? Well, they want this place. I had Brad do a quick check, and it looks like they can qualify for the mortgage loan on this amount."

Nancy took the papers when she reached the porch, and looked at them. "This is awfully low, isn't it?"

"The market is tight, Fancy Nancy, and this is the only offer we've had. There's no sense in countering, because those kids don't have more than this. I say, take it and run."

"Well, I'll have to talk it over with Kip."

"Why?"

"Because he's the man of the family," she said firmly.

"That's nuts, but okay. We have seventy-two hours to respond. Don't take that long. Call me tomorrow." He turned as a car pulled in behind Nancy's. "Fletcher McGill. I heard you were seeing him. Going for the gusto, huh, Fancy Nancy? Planning on living on the McGill estate? Don't count on it. Fletch will cut out of Oakville again soon. He'll never settle down."

"I'll call you tomorrow, Hank," Nancy said. Her gaze was riveted on Fletcher as he walked slowly toward them.

"Hi, there, Fletch," Hank said. "I just sold Fancy Nancy's house for her. Well, I will have sold it, once she signs the papers. She says she has to talk to Kip, because he's the man of the family."

"He is," Fletcher said, his jaw tight as he stepped onto the porch. "And I suggest you remember that in case you run into Kip, Bloom."

"Oh. Well. Sure thing," Hank said, backing off the porch. "Fine boy . . . um, man of the family, that Kip. Call me tomorrow, Fancy Nancy." He hurried to his car.

"What a creep," Fletcher said. "Why did you list the house with him?"

"It was him or Cleve Smith. They're the only two realtors left in Oakville."

"Cleve Smith thinks he's God's gift to women."

"And he has very busy hands. Hank is the lesser of two evils. Better to deal with a Smurf than an octopus."

"Yeah," Fletcher said, slowly shifting his gaze to meet hers. "Hello, Nance," he said quietly, not smiling.

"Hi," she said, attempting a smile that failed. "You look tired."

"I've . . . had a rotten headache all day."

"Are you getting the flu?"

"No, I got drunk, totally smashed, sitting right in the McGill living room."

"Why?"

He shrugged. "It seemed like a good idea at the time."

"Were you celebrating? I mean, I assume you told your parents your news about being David Forester."

"Yeah, I told them, and they're pleased, very proud. But, no, I wasn't celebrating."

"Oh," she said. Then why had he gotten drunk? What was he trying to escape from? Should she ask? Wait for him to tell her? Darn, walking on eggshells like this was hard on the nerves. *She* had a rotten headache, too, now that she thought about it, but the cause of hers was standing right in front of her. "Let's go inside," she said, fishing in her purse for her keys.

In the living room, Nancy turned to face Fletcher,wishing he'd smile, wishing he'd take her in his arms and hold her, kiss her. Wishing he'd do anything but just stand there staring at her with an expression on his face that she couldn't even come close to reading.

"Well," she said, forcing a lightness to her voice, "let's see what this contract is all about." She sat down on the sofa. "Care to sit down, Fletcher?" she asked, her nose buried in the papers. He sat next to her. "Do you know anything about this stuff?"

He leaned over her shoulder and looked at the forms. "It's pretty standard. The question is whether or not you want to sell at that price."

Oh, he smelled so good. And the heat. How could one man generate so much heat? "Hank had a point. This is the only offer we've had. We've lived in this house since I was born, so we'll make a fairly decent profit. I'll put it in a fund for Kip. Then, heaven forbid, if anything happens to his scholarship he'll still have college money."

"What about you?"

Yes, darn it, good question, Nancy thought. What about her? She'd assumed she'd be discussing wedding plans with Fletcher by now. Maybe she'd put the ball back in his court. "What about me?" she asked, turning to look at him. That was a mistake, Nancy, she told herself. There he was, so close, so very close. There were those lips . . .

On hers.

It was a hard kiss, a searing kiss, as Fletcher sank his hands into Nancy's curls and held her head.

A groan rumbled up from Fletcher's throat as he drank of her sweetness, savored her taste and aroma, the feel of her breasts crushed against his chest.

Nance.

Through the hours of the day, with his head pounding like a tormenting jackhammer, he'd tried to think, to sort things through. He'd remembered his father's words, which he'd heard through his drunken stupor, saying that he wasn't giving Nancy enough credit; to look to the future, not the past; to find his happiness in the tomorrows.

But his head had throbbed, increasing his confusion and fear, and he'd felt as though it had been a million years since he'd held his Nancy in his arms.

Fletcher drew a quick, ragged breath, then claimed her mouth again in a desperate attempt to free himself of his raging thoughts and just feel. Heat curled and coiled deep within him, gathering low in his body, stirring his manhood, until he ached for fulfillment, for release from the wanting of the only woman he'd ever loved.

"Nancy," he murmured close to her lips, "I want you. I want you now."

"Yes," she whispered. "Oh, yes, Fletcher, I want you, too, but Kip will be home any minute."

"Hell," he said, then moved her gently away from him. He turned to rest his elbows on his knees, making a steeple of his fingers as he willed his body back under control.

Nancy placed her hand on her heart and swallowed heavily. "Whew."

"Yeah," Fletcher said gruffly, not turning to look at her. "I'm a little old for making out on the sofa, then being told to forget it, go take a cold shower."

"I can't help it, Fletcher. Kip lives here too. I won't have him come home to find me locked in the bedroom making mad, passionate love. It just wouldn't be right."

"I know that," he said, sinking back against the cushions. He turned his head to look at her. "My mind knows it. My body thinks it's a crock." He smiled. "Can I help it if you're a very sexy lady? I kiss you, I'm gone."

"I'm flattered, sir," she said, batting her eyelashes at him. Well, glory be, he'd smiled. No, now he was frowning again. That was the quickest smile on record.

"Are you going to sign that contract?" he asked.

"I'll show it to Kip, just as I told Hank, but I imagine I will."

"Then you'll be all set to move to Atlanta after Kip graduates."

"Yes."

"With me," he said, looking directly into her eyes.

Time stopped. Time just stopped, and with it, Nancy was sure, her heart. She knew she wasn't breathing, and was positive that her heart as well had come to a screeching halt.

"I"—she drew in a gulp of air—"beg your pardon?"

"I want us to be together. I want to make love to you at night, wake up next to you in the morning, make love to you again. I know that job you have waiting for you is important to you. You worked hard to teach yourself computer skills. I can understand that, because I taught myself all I know about photography. Do you want to be with me, Nance?"

"Yes, of course I do, but—" Were they talking marriage here? Exactly what was Fletcher saying? Should she ask? What did sophisticated people do under circumstances like this? "You'd work on your book?"

"That's stalled at the moment. Selene called me just before I came over here. She went back to New York this morning and had a meeting with the publisher. She's still negotiating the contract."

"Oh, I thought you'd already signed it."

"Nope."

"So what would you do in Atlanta?"

He grinned. "Make love to you."

"Fletcher, be serious."

"Believe me, Nance, making love to you is a very serious business. And very special, and very beautiful." He leaned toward her. "And I want you right this minute."

"Fletcher," she said, pushing against his chest. "I can't think when you do that."

"Don't think. Just take off your clothes."

"Fletcher!"

"Damn," he said, moving back again. "All right." He paused. "Do you figure Kip would go to the movies if I gave him twenty bucks. He could see the great ant flick."

"Oh, for Pete's sake," Nancy said, laughing. The ant wasn't so bad. Kip might like that ant. Oh, Nancy, stop it. "What would you do in Atlanta . . . when you weren't ravishing my body?"

"Nancy, when I first started messing around with that camera, I'd have the film developed for me. That didn't go well later, because I only wanted the faces, and I knew where I wanted the negatives cropped. So I taught myself how to develop my own film. Sometimes I'd have to wait until I could get to a place large enough to have a studio I could rent that was set up with what I needed. When I got my ankle creamed I was behind—had a lot of film waiting to be developed. I still have it. A buddy of mine is holding it in the Phillipines, along with four very expensive cameras of mine."

"I see."

"If we got a big enough place, I could set up my own darkroom, buy my own equipment, and tackle the work that's stacked up."

"Before the book."

He leaned his head back on the top of the sofa and stared at the ceiling. "Yes," he said quietly, "the wonderful book that will bring Fletcher McGill front-row center. Fletcher McGill and his pal David Forester." A muscle jerked in his jaw. He looked at her again. "The book will take months to do, and that was what I wanted, because I was tired of traveling alone, being alone. This is good, Nance, don't you see? You'll have your job at Cory Computer, I'll be busy, and we'll be together."

Married together? Living-together together? What was he saying? Nancy asked herself again. Oh, this was ridiculous. They weren't discussing what was for dinner. This was important.

"Fletcher, are you planning on marrying me?" Oh, Lord. Oh, merciful heaven. Somebody tell her she hadn't said that.

"Holy smokes," Kip said, coming into the living room from the kitchen, "I can't believe you said that."

"Oh, damn," Nancy said, clamping her hand over her eyes.

"Tsk, tsk," Kip said. "And now she's swearing, too. As the man of the family, Nancy, I must say that I'm very surprised at you. First you boldly and brashly ask this fine southern gentleman if he plans to marry you. Since when did you get so liberated? Then you—"

"Kip!" Nancy yelled, dropping her hand from her eyes. "Go to your room."

"Not on your life," he said, flopping into a chair. "I wouldn't miss this for the world." He flapped his hand at them. "Carry on. I'll just take notes. I won't say a word."

Speak, McGill, Fletcher told himself frantically. Say something. He'd wanted to marry Nancy ever since that summer six year earlier, ever since Fletcher's Pond. But something had happened to him at the moment she'd declared her love for him in that room in the gallery in Atlanta. He'd been hinting that they should just live together in Atlanta because that damn icy fist of fear was holding him more and more tightly . . .

Out of order, his mind taunted. She'd said she loved him out of order!

He didn't care, his heart whispered in reply. Not at that moment, not right now. Not while sitting there next to her, having just held and kissed her. Not while picturing creating a home with her, being with her every day and every night in Atlanta. Not while she was gazing at him with her great big blue eyes, her face flushed with embarrassment because she'd blurted out her question regarding his intentions. He loved her so much.

"I do declare, Miss Forest," he drawled in an exaggerated southern accent, "that it would be the right and fittin' thing for y'all to do, seein' how we just spent a compromisin' weekend together in Atlanta. Yes, ma'am, I truly do believe y'all should marry me 'fore this here young master comes after me with a shotgun."

"Hear, hear," Kip said, grinning broadly.

"Oh, Fletcher, hush," Nancy said, whopping him on the arm. "I'm embarrassed enough." She got to her feet. "I'm going to start dinner. You're welcome to stay and eat with us."

Fletcher reached out and grabbed her hand. "Nancy," he said, his tone and expression serious now. "I'm sincerely asking you, here, in this home, in front of your brother, whom I respect very much, if you will marry me." He got to his feet. "I'm asking you to be my wife, my partner, my other half. I love you more than I can say in words. Will you, Nance? Will you marry me?"

"Wow," Kip whispered, his eyes wide. "Awesome."

"Fletcher, I . . ." Nancy stopped speaking as tears filled her eyes.

"Please?"

"Yes," she said, flinging herself into his arms. "Oh, yes, I'll marry you, Fletcher. I love you so very, very much."

Fletcher kissed her.

"Wow," Kip said again.

Fletcher lifted his head. "When?"

"When what?" Nancy said dreamily.

"When will you marry me?"

"Oh, well, I—I don't know. I mean, I don't want a lot of hoopla, just family." Her eyes widened. "Family. Oh, heavens, yours is going to have a fit. I'm not the kind of woman they would want a McGill to marry."

Fletcher's eyes flashed with instant anger. "Don't say that. Don't even think it."

"That's right," Kip said decisively, but no one paid any attention to him.

"Have you got that, Nance?" Fletcher asked.

"But—"

"No, it won't even be discussed." He put his arm around her shoulders and turned to face Kip. "What do you think, Kip? Should we do this number before you leave, so you can give the bride away?"

Kip got to this feet. "Oh, yeah, that would be great. I'd really like to be there."

"Fair enough," Fletcher said, nodding. "I'd prefer not to be married with a cast on my leg. That's tacky. So is that our target date? I get the cast off, and we tie the knot. Okay, Nance?"

"Okay," she said, smiling up at him.

"We three are going out to dinner," Fletcher said. "Oakville is not the celebration center of the world, but it will have to do. Kip, you can drive my car."

"Drive your . . . Drive that . . . Wow!"

Fletcher tossed him the keys. "Go warm it up."

After Kip had run out the front door, Fletcher turned Nancy toward him and tilted her chin up with one long finger.

"I probably blew it," he said, "proposing to you in front of Kip." He cleared his throat. "Nancy, will you marry me?"

"Yes," she whispered.

"You're sure?"

"Are you, Fletcher?"

Out of order! his mind raged.

Shut up, McGill, he mentally roared.

"Yes, Nancy, I'm sure. I love you."

"And I love you."

"Then I'd say, sweet Nance," he said, lowering his head toward hers, "that we've got it made." His mouth met hers. Had it made, he mentally repeated. If the demons didn't win. If this chill of fear didn't freeze his heart. If—

Kip honked the horn.

Fletcher lifted his head and chuckled. "The master's voice, darlin', is callin'," he drawled. "Let's go. By the way, where do you want to get married?"

"At Fletcher's Pond."

"Ah, Nance," he said, trailing his thumb over her

cheek, "that is the nicest place you could have picked. Thank you. I'm going to make you happy, Nancy. I swear to you, I'm going to make you happy."

And Fletcher did make her happy.

At first.

The following weeks flew by, and it seemed to Nancy that there weren't enough hours in the day to accomplish all that needed to be done. She and Fletcher spent another weekend in Atlanta, apartment hunting, and to their delight found a large, sunny place that met their needs perfectly. They were to have all new furniture, Fletcher insisted, and yet another trip was made to shop.

A family dinner party was held at the McGill estate, and Nancy was convinced that she would die of nervousness before she could even arrive in her peach-yogurt dress.

To her amazement and relief, she and Kip were warmly welcomed, and Dennis McGill made a toast to the future happiness of the bride and groom. Fletcher's mouth dropped open when Shane launched into an animated discussion with Kip about baseball. Shane knew the batting averages of nearly every major-league player, and Kip was in awe. The evening was a huge success. Elsie asked permission to release an announcement of the pending wedding to the newspaper, and by late the next afternoon the town of Oakville, Georgia, was in a tizzy.

It was fun, busy, exhausting, and Nancy was sure her genuine smile stayed in place even while she slept. She loved and was loved in return by the most magnificent man in the world. She had a new extended family, which had received her into its warm embrace. She was inching closer and closer to a glorious future with Fletcher that was even beyond her fantasies.

Fletcher's cast was removed. He was given a clean bill of health and a set of exercises to do to strengthen his ankle.

And then the wedding.

Shane, Fletcher had told Nancy, was up to something, and the something brought tears to Nancy's eyes when they arrived for the simple ceremony. The tall grass by Fletcher's Pond had been mowed, and a multitude of fragrant flowers in baskets filled the area. And there, in fairyland splendor, was a white gazebo by the edge of the pond. Nancy Forest became Mrs. Fletcher McGill while standing in the enchanting gazebo with sunlight pouring over the assembled group.

At the reception on the estate, Elsie and Dennis gave the newlyweds their wedding present: the title to the land containing Fletcher's Pond and five acres surrounding it.

The morning after Kip's graduation, Nancy and Fletcher took Kip to the airport. Nancy smiled, hugged Kip, hugged him some more, and kept smiling. The moment the plane left the ground, Nancy flung herself into Fletcher's arms and wept for the next half hour as he led her from the airport to the car, a soft smile on his face.

There wasn't time for an official honeymoon trip, because Nancy was due to report to Cory Computer. Fletcher gave her a string of delicate pearls and a note that said, "IOU one honeymoon trip to the place of your choosing." Nancy cried again, and said she had used up a year's quota of tears.

And they made love. At night, at dawn, in Nancy's bed in the little house, in the gazebo at their very own Fletcher's Pond, they made love. The burning desire to be one seemed to grow stronger with each passing day. They reached for each other eagerly, giving, taking, rejoicing in their union.

It was glorious, all of it. Nancy felt at times that she would burst with the sheer joy of being alive and so incredibly happy. With a quiet good-bye for the years spent there, she locked the door for the last time on the little house, and drove with her husband toward Atlanta and their new life together.

The first few weeks in Atlanta were hectic. Nancy's head was buzzing when she returned home from work each day as she tried to grasp the routine of her job. Fletcher was busy tracking down the finest equipment available, for the darkroom he was creating in the second bedroom. Spare time was spent shopping for the final touches needed to make their apartment homey. And they made love. Passion flared at a touch, a smile, an accidental brushing against the other. They closed the door on the world and became one.

Then suddenly it was very quiet.

It took Nancy nearly a full week to realize that the flurry of nonstop activity was over. They had fallen into a pattern for their days and nights. She left the apartment before Fletcher was awake, came home to find him in the darkroom. She prepared dinner, he helped her clean up, they spent a quiet evening reading or watching television, then went to bed, where they made sweet love.

Another uneventful week passed, during which Nancy woke on two nights to find Fletcher standing naked by the window, staring out over the sleeping city. She hadn't gone to him on either occasion, sensing a wall of tension around him that virtually shouted at her that he wanted to be alone.

Fletcher began to spend longer hours in the darkroom. He responded to Nancy's knock at the door and said he'd be right out to have dinner, but then wouldn't appear. Three times during the following week she ate alone. He mumbled his excuses when he emerged, said it wouldn't happen again, then repeated the performance the next night.

Nancy began to sleep restlessly as nightmares plagued her. She had the same dream night after night. Fletcher was leaving, always leaving. He'd smile at her sadly, shake his head, then go. Sometimes he walked away, other nights he was in his car, and in one horror-filled dream, he rode off on the giant ant. But he always left her standing alone, with tears streaming down her face.

The tension in the McGill home grew.

The silence screamed.

To add to Nancy's generally dismal state of mind, she came to the private conclusion that she absolutely hated her job. The spiel they had given her when they'd hired her was, in short, she decided, a bunch of bull. She hadn't been near a computer more than three times, and felt she was nothing more than a glorified gofer. She ran off thousands of copies of everyone else's work, punched cute little holes and placed the papers in colored binders, was loaned a company car—oh, whoop-de-do—to deliver reports to customers. And, *and*, she silently fumed, she was in charge of making the coffee.

She longed to pour out her woes about Cory Computer to Fletcher, ask his advice, soak up a little sympathy. Even more, she yearned to ask him what was wrong with *him*, why he spent more and more time closed up in the darkroom, why he hardly spoke during the remaining hours of the evening, why the solitary vigils by the window were becoming a nightly ritual. Driving home from work, Nancy would practice her speech, her approach to Fletcher, to bring everything to the surface so they could discuss it. But when she saw the tight set to his jaw, the distant, cool look in his eyes, she lost her nerve.

The tension grew, and Nancy's heart was slowly breaking.

On the night of their three-month anniversary, Nancy prepared a special dinner, complete with candlelight. She'd dashed out on her lunch hour and bought a powder-blue full-length satin hostess gown that clung to her soft curves. She sprayed a delicate cologne in strategic places, took a deep breath, and knocked on the darkroom door.

"Yes?"

"Fletcher? Dinner is ready."

"Yeah, okay. Give me a minute."

"Can you come now? Everything is waiting."

"Yeah, yeah, fine."

Ten minutes later, she knocked again.

"What!"

"Fletcher, please come to dinner. This is a special occasion."

The door was flung open. "It is?" he asked. "What special"— his gaze raked over her—"occasion?"

"It's our three-month anniversary."

"Oh. I like that whatever-it-is-you're wearing."

"Thank you."

"Let me wash my hands, and I'll be right there."

Fletcher joined her at the table minutes later, and raised his eyebrows as he saw the candles.

"I didn't know I was supposed to do something special for a three-month anniversary," he said. "I blew it, huh?"

"No," she said, smiling. "I just felt like doing this. Did you read Kip's letter? He sounds very happy."

"Yeah, he's doing great. This is delicious food, Nance."

"Thank you." They ate in silence for several minutes. "So, Fletcher," she said, forcing a lightness to her voice, "what do you hear from Selene? You haven't mentioned her or the book in weeks."

Fletcher's head snapped up, and he looked at her with such sudden anger, she nearly dropped her fork. Her heart beat wildly and a knot tightened in her stomach as she stared at him.

"I wondered how long it would take," he said, his voice so chilling, Nancy hardly recognized it.

"What?" she whispered, totally confused. Dear heaven, she thought frantically, his eyes were like chips of ice. What was wrong with him?

"What's the matter, Nancy?" he asked, a bitter edge to his voice. "Is married life with Fletcher McGill too dull for you? Are you eager to get to the flash and dash that will come with David Forester?"

"No. I was just making conversation. I thought Selene would have worked out the details of the contract by now, that's all."

Fletcher pushed his plate away. "I hate to disappoint you, but it's all on hold. The editor she was working with was called away on a family emergency. She prefers to wait and finish negotiations with him when he gets back."

"Fine," Nancy said, raising her hands.

"Is it?" he asked, a pulse beating rapidly in his temple. "Or are you gritting your teeth because you're stuck in this drab routine longer than you expected? I live here, remember? I've seen the changes in you. You hardly smile anymore."

"Have you bothered to wonder why?" she asked, her voice rising.

"I don't have to . . . I already know. It was a package deal. With Fletcher McGill you got David Forester and the world he offered. You resent the hell out of the fact that David Forester is taking his own sweet time about showing up."

Nancy's eyes widened in shock. "I can't believe you're saying these things. You're talking about David Forester as though he were a real man, a separate person from you."

"Isn't he?" he asked, his voice ominously low. "Isn't that who you stood with in that gallery that night and said you loved? Isn't it, Nancy?"

Oh, dear God, no! Strange black dots danced before Nancy's eyes. It was all falling into place. The skein of tangled yarn had been set to rights, but the picture it created was wrong! She had waited too long to tell Fletcher that she loved him. The demon within him was his doubt of *her!* Oh, Fletcher, no.

He got to his feet and walked to the window, bracing his hands on the frame. His body was rigid, his anger and hurt seeming to crackle through the air, making it difficult for Nancy to breathe.

A rush of panic swept over her. She didn't know what to do or say to convince Fletcher he was so very wrong. If only she'd told him minutes sooner, that she loved him, none of this would be happening. Minutes, little ticking seconds on a clock, were destroying everything they had together.

"Did you think," he asked, his voice flat, "that I wouldn't notice it was all out of order? Your declaration of love . . . was out of order. Too late. It came too late. You said it to David Forester, not Fletcher McGill." He turned slowly to face her, and Nancy saw such raw pain in his dark eyes that a sob caught in her throat. "I pushed it away," he went on, "pretended it wasn't true, because I loved you so much, needed you so damn much. But I've seen the changes in you in the past weeks. I know you're not happy with Fletcher McGill, with just me."

A strange fury erupted in Nancy, born of fear and nerves stretched to the limit. She smacked the table with her hand and got quickly to her feet, blue eyes flashing with anger.

"Damn right I'm not happy with Fletcher McGill," she said. "And I'm going to spell out for you exactly why I'm not."

"I already know!"

"The hell you do. Listen to me, McGill, but this time *hear* what I'm saying. I'm miserable because my husband has become a sullen recluse who hides in a darkroom, then hardly speaks to me when he comes out. I also hate my job, but you wouldn't know that, because you've been too busy wallowing in self-pity to notice."

"You hate your job? I thought you—"

"Shut up. You've been watching, waiting, making me pass tests for you all these weeks, you crumb, and now you've decided I've failed. Well, guess what, McGill? *You* failed *me.*"

"What?"

"You failed to believe in me and my love, Fletcher," she said, her voice starting to tremble. "I said that I loved you out of order? Okay, maybe it seemed that way, but didn't you hear the rest? Oh, God, Fletcher, didn't you hear me say *I'd never stopped loving you?* You. Fletcher McGill, of Fletcher's Pond. You. Not David Forester." Tears spilled onto her cheeks.

"Nance—" He took a step toward her.

"Don't do the book," she said, backing away from him. "Please, Fletcher? I love you so much. Don't let David Forester take it all away from us." She swept the tears from her cheeks. "You said you were tired of traveling alone. I could go with you. Please?" She was sobbing. "Can't it be just the two of us for now? Please, Fletcher?"

"Oh, God." He groaned. He closed the distance between them and pulled her roughly into his arms. "What have I done? What have I done to you, to us, to all we had? The fear . . . Oh, Nance, it grew so big, it was so cold, so cold, and I was so afraid." He framed her face in his hands and lifted her head to meet her gaze. Tears glistened in his eyes. "I'm so sorry, Nance," he said, is voice choked with emotion. "Please forgive me."

"Fletcher—"

"We'll take a year, okay? I'll show you wonderful places and incredible faces. It'll just be the two of us. Then we'll see, we'll talk about it, decide together if we're ready to have David Forester in our lives. Okay, Nance? Okay?"

She smiled through her tears. "Oh, yes, Fletcher, it's more than okay. It's perfect."

"You were right. I listened, yet I didn't hear you, and I'm so very sorry. But the demons are gone. We beat them, Nance. We did it together."

"I love you, Fletcher."

"And I love you, Nance." He pulled her close and held her, simply held her, for a long, special moment. "Come into the bedroom with me, darling," he finally said.

"Why?"

He gripped her shoulders and moved her back to grin down at her. "Why? Why? she asks. What a silly question."

"So answer it," she said, matching his smile.

He swung her up into his arms, his eyes filled with the messages of love and need and want.

"We're going to play checkers, of course," he said, striding across the room.

"Of course," she said, laughing, her heart nearly bursting with love.

Bursting with love for Fletcher.

Fletcher McGill, of Fletcher's Pond.

THE EDITOR'S CORNER

It's not easy handling six spirited heroines and six "to die for" handsome, sexy heroes each month, but it's fun trying. It's a tough job, but someone has to do it! The truth is there's nothing tough about editing these LOVESWEPTs—our authors are a joy to work with. What's tough is knowing which book to read first! Luckily, we've solved that problem for you by numbering the books. So once again we have six books that explore romance in all its forms—steamy, sensuous, sweet, funny, and heartwarming.

Our first LOVESWEPT for the month, #240 **CAJUN NIGHTS** by Susan Richardson is definitely steamy! It's set in the bayous of Louisiana where our heroine, renowned travel writer Jeannie Kilmartin, is looking for the perfect hideaway for her next story. Instead, she finds dark, brooding Elliot Escudier poling through the water on his handmade boat. Jeannie has to look twice as Elliot appears in the marshes—is he some long lost pirate who's come to claim her? Elliot owns the land that Jeannie is writing about and he's come to claim the land and keep her from printing her article. And he'll do anything to stop her. Jeannie doesn't mind his interference because she adores his dark, sexy looks. Eventually, all thoughts of an article are thrown out the window when the lovers finally succumb to their overwhelming desire.

In **TRAVELIN' MAN** by Charlotte Hughes, LOVESWEPT #241, Dannie Drysdale is whimsical and luscious looking and utterly determined not to fall in love with a traveling man because at last she's put down roots. Brian Anthony is one extraordinary fellow—as handsome as he is sensitive! But alas, he's a salesman on the move who's determined to rise to the top of the corporate ladder. Nothing can stand in his way or keep him in one place for long. Except Dannie! Once Dannie's eccentric father throws the lovers together, Brian's goals change. Then Dannie's resistance is finally broken down by a bad case of chickenpox and by the great guy who's nursing her back to health. The travelin' man and the

(continued)

"stay-put" woman realize that they both want the same thing—each other!

Something funny happened at LOVESWEPT this month—we discovered we had two heroes with the same name. You probably think that the hero's name is John or Joe or Tom, Dick or Harry—a common name that could easily be duplicated. But then you know that our heroes are never common so they never have common names. Can you believe that we have two strong, sexy, devastating Lincolns this month? Well, we do and we'll let you decide which one is more lovable, but we know that's going to be a very tough decision.

In **INTIMATE DETAILS,** by Barbara Boswell, LOVESWEPT #242, Lincoln Scott is the man Vanessa Ramsey's father decides she should marry. Lincoln finds the dazzling temptress a delectable challenge, especially since she won't consider even liking Linc—and her father's interference has turned her into a tigress! But Vanessa finds it harder and harder to ignore Lincoln's dreamboat looks and his fierce caresses. When he touches her heart, Vanessa listens to her feelings and for the first time in her life, she lets herself be loved. There are some of Barbara's wittiest scenes in this delightful love story—such as one in which her father tries to justify his actions and digs himself into a hole a mile deep. Unforgettable.

Joan Elliott Pickart's offering for the month is **KISS ME AGAIN, SAM,** LOVESWEPT #243, a wonderfully humorous and heartwarming romance in which the heroine appears for the first time hanging from the rafters! Read on and find out how she got there and you'll discover that Austin Tyler is a very pretty auburn-haired construction worker hired to repair Sam Carter's house. Sam finds Austin irresistible in both body and mind and he tells her so. But Austin is afraid that once she tells Sam her terrible secret, he won't want her anymore. Could he make her believe that everything about her was precious to him and he loved all the woman she was?

SAPPHIRE LIGHTNING by Fayrene Preston, LOVESWEPT #244 features our second hero named Linc and I must admit I'm torn between the two men! Linc Sinclair

(continued)

is a handsome, healthy jogger with a fantastic body, as well as being a successful businessman with a fabulous art collection. Toni Sinclair was married to his cousin who died accidentally and now that Toni is on her own with her six-month-old son, she's decided never to remarry. She wasn't a great wife the first time around, and she doesn't want to risk failing again. Linc throws a party in her honor welcoming Toni to the family's hometown and while at his house, Toni realizes just how much they have in common. It all begins with a love for art—and ends with Linc's love for one particular beautiful, female artist. Fayrene Preston has once again set a sensuous, romantic scene where two lovers destined for one another will be sure to find their hearts' desires.

Deborah Smith is a new LOVESWEPT author and we're very excited about **JED'S SWEET REVENGE,** LOVESWEPT #245, the story of a sun-bronzed cowboy and the beautiful woman he calls "Wildflower"! Jed Powers leaves Wyoming and heads south for Sancia Island to finally seek his revenge on his dead grandfather. Instead he finds Thena Saint-Colbet—very much alive and a gorgeous free spirit with wild, thick auburn hair. Thena lives on the island that Jed intends to destroy, and she teaches him its beauty. All thought of revenge fades when love takes its place and, in the end, Jed's revenge is sweet.

I'm sure you're going to enjoy Deborah Smith's book and welcome her to the LOVESWEPT family. You have a wonderful month of reading ahead of you, so stay warm and cozy with your favorite LOVESWEPT.

Sincerely,

Kate Hartson

Kate Hartson
Editor
LOVESWEPT
Bantam Books, Inc.
666 Fifth Avenue
New York, NY 10103

☐ *YORK, THE RENEGADE by Iris Johansen*

Some men were made to fight dragons, Sierra Smith thought when she first met York Delaney. The rebel brother had roamed the world for years before calling the rough mining town of Hell's Bluff home. Now, the spirited young woman who'd penetrated this renegade's paradise had awakened a savage and tender possessiveness in York: something he never expected to find in himself. Sierra had known loneliness and isolation too—enough to realize that York's restlessness had only to do with finding a place to belong. Could she convince him that love was such a place, that the refuge he'd always sought was in her arms?

(21847 • $2.75)

☐ *BURKE, THE KINGPIN by Fayrene Preston*

Cara Winston appeared as a fantasy, racing on horseback to catch the day's last light—her silver hair glistening, her dress the color of the Arizona sunset . . . and Burke Delaney wanted her. She was on his horse, on his land: she would have to belong to him too. But Cara was quicksilver, impossible to hold, a wild creature whose scent was midnight flowers and sweet grass. Burke had always taken what he wanted, by willing it or fighting for it; Cara cherished her freedom and refused to believe his love would last. Could he make her see he'd captured her to have and hold forever?

(21848 • $2.75)